Economy an

By

The Shadow

Table of Contents

Introduction

I dedicate this book to all my fellow human beings on Earth with the hope of giving them an insight into the key areas that would affect their happiness throughout their lifelong journey, from birth to their death. In doing so, I would attempt to prompt them to look deeply into the factors that could affect their happiness, leading to a true evaluation of their emotions in this journey we call life.

These factors primarily are the ones associated with their faith or beliefs, such as do's & don'ts they dictate, followed by rules of the society they live in or, in other words, the Culture, the Economy, and family values. However, they may not be what they should be, but it is there solely for the survival of the community only or the safety of its members. As an example, there may be rules in the society that tell its people to worship some object placed in the village to realize all their needs or the safety of its people by virtue of the power of that object or what it represents, which is expected to lead good or 100% economy of that society.

Once we are adults, we now have a few options here. We could go by such rules without questioning the validity of these beliefs or question the same and not accept it as a correct belief if this society does not have a good economy currently for all its people. On the other hand, if the economy is 100% and everybody in the society is happy, this questioning would not matter, which is not the case with any society or community of people I currently know of that has enough to eat, no sickness, no death, etc.

Or question it and not accept or accept it as a true belief. To this end, in situations where it really matters to one's life, it is prudent to rationalize such beliefs via our own mind with information at hand or by research-backed by one's own experiences, which could lead to the path of true knowledge which may lead to good or 100% economy for oneself. Hence, consideration must be given to constraints imposed by society or what is dictated at birth when looking for what is the truth that possibly could make one's economy 100% or at the very least near to it in this world.

In this regard, we find the economy to be an important driver responsible for causing poverty, hunger, sickness, family issues, monetary issues, social issues, even global issues within the society we live in. Then one may attempt to withstand the pain and suffering caused by these events now in the belief of a next life where such would not happen to him or her, but all whims provided for or 100% economic status for eternity.

Unfortunately, beliefs do not help us to find solutions to such situations consistently. For example, if you believe in a supernatural power, it may be of help if it exists and if it has power over humans in a good or bad way. As such, parents of a dying child may pray to whatever supernatural power they believe, and the child may miraculously recover. However, this does not mean that all the sick children would get better in a similar manner even if their parents follow the same beliefs and same devotions or even a higher religious observance. If this is the case, as an example, there would be no need for cancer hospitals for the children as all the parents would devotedly follow the faith of the parents of the ones who got healed from an incurable disease, without question.

Yet, if we have a true understanding as an individual of what is going on around us or what we are subjected to, as mentioned above, then we would be free of desires, attachments, lust, and greed. This is necessary in order to be liberated from pain and suffering or to be in peace and contentment with one's current circumstances. Moreover, by virtue of true understanding of the aforesaid as the reason for our desires, one would be able to face whatever calamity that befalls them. However, at the same time, it would be particularly important to prevent any such misfortune if one can be invigorated to achieve better economic stability for tomorrow for self and every living being with mercy and compassion.

So, let us look at these aspects of our lives by evaluating things such as evolution, birth, family, society, politics, religion or beliefs, animal world, old age, sickness, and even the universe or space. Then, of course, we cannot ignore the possibility of the existence of heaven or hell either as faith in these have a possibility of directly or indirectly affecting our happiness or wellbeing in this life now. Or possibly a next life.

We need to bear in mind that the primary tools we use for this purpose are our senses and our trained mind. One can disseminate information mainly by experience or education to make rational deductions. As an example, seeing a fire, we would not know if it would burn if touched. However, we tend to believe this to be true if this has been told to us by others who have experienced the same and have proven to be people of integrity, honesty, or who have the best interest for humanity. Hence, we consider such to be true, even if we personally do not experience the same.

Keep in mind that we can be misled on the effects of the fire if the intent of the first person sharing this information was to convince us that this fire does not burn even if it does. For example, a king may say to his subjects that whoever opposes him will go to hell as he is the only person that God selected to be the king or queen of his people. Now, opposing him would be the same as opposing God. And for that, he or she will even assert the punishment that is going to be meted out now for that person as death by beheading would be nothing compared to what is going to happen in the next life for that person, meaning it would be torture inclusive. Indeed, a terrifying prospect at the hand of that God.

Therefore, it is observed that we can easily be misled for another person's own benefit, or this could even be for a good cause as to keep the human-animal in good behavior for the benefit of the economic conditions of the masses. For example, a king or queen would issue a warning to his people to be weary of fraudsters when conducting their economic and, in return, rob them in another way through higher taxes in order to pay for their own pleasures. And this may not even be king or a queen, but people appointed by people to govern them.

In this type of world, where possible, it is better to know something to be true as per our own experience if this is of major concern to oneself. Then one may argue, we cannot know everything but must rely on what others say initially. Nevertheless, this does not stop us from digging deeper for the true understanding of key issues affecting our life if one is already suffering because of one's current economic state.

In this regard, the author does not intend to be biased to any religion, philosophy, political system, or any other factor but to present the facts as he sees them. He expects the reader to use the author's thinking at his or her own discretion but with an open mind. In the end, the reader may also consider this information as pure garbage or information for further thought. In case it is the latter, to challenge one's own mind with this direction of thinking for further research by themselves.

To this end, this is the author's attempt to find facts without prejudice and not to bring disrepute to any belief. The author once again requests the reader to have an open mind while reading this book. In the end, to have an affirmation of what the reader currently believes or to seek more information to validate his current beliefs. If not to look at other beliefs to seek answers to his or her pain and sufferings to make his or her economic conditions better.

Hence, the book has been titled **"Economy and Beliefs"** as through this book you would see the profound effect the Economy can have on our Spirituality or Faith or Beliefs. Strong faith in whatever the beliefs would allow people to withstand whatever pain and suffering they are faced with now with hope for 100% economic condition in the next life in heaven bestowed by their God for unwavering belief in him. As per current beliefs, this may be faith in a God or for some Nirvana, and for the atheist, it does not matter as there is no life after death.

Chapter 1: Evolution

Early humans lived in caves. They had an easygoing life as far as their economy went. Their main concern was food without any frills, meaning considerably basic naturally roasted food. They hunted with wooden spears or rocks with no clothing or minimal clothing to cover them and lived in a land that provided sufficient food, fruits from plants, and meat from animals. Sometimes they died when the availability of such food disappeared due to drought or other natural occurrences. Some learned to migrate to other areas where food was available to survive when it was possible. However, in general, their economy could have been average as we in the advance economic society would also try out their style of living as doing our famous barbecues or eating meat that we call rare, medium-rare, or somewhat raw.

Now we have upgraded ourselves from an easygoing and extremely basic economy of eating what is available domestically and being in harmony with the environment without pesticides or plastic to a complex society full of artificial substances for our sustenance.

We now manipulate our environment to provide for our needs by poisoning and denying the same resources for future generations. Society has evolved to using chemical-induced artificial fertilizers to grow food, thereby poisoning our drinking water. Tapping the deep groundwater with machinery to grow food in the desert causes the water table to drop and reduces water supply to other areas. This results in a loss of drinking water for the people living in these areas.

The key aspect I see in this regard is what we call the civilized existence of humans; meaning, covered up humans living in houses or shelters at the least, while their ancestors, most probably the apes, were hanging around naked in the forest still. The birth of shame would have contributed to this critical factor to cover themselves, and this could have been the seed of what we now call civilized society. The shame does not mean bad conduct but the smell of excretion from all the openings in our bodies.

There are many other theories as to how we came into existence. One school of thought says this is by an intelligent creator, where we do not know who created the Creator. However, on the other hand, some would say the Creator did not need a creator. Then from the reasoning power of our mind, the question would be, did our world too then need a creator?

Considering the theory of the Creator, a rationale drawn in its favor is that at our birth, we need to have some pre-programming already inbuilt into us to sustain life. For example, a newborn mammal, such as elephants, lions, tigers, humans, etc., would need to know how to suckle the mother for sustenance at birth, or else it would die. Additionally, another example would be of birds having the knowledge to build complex nests to bring up their young. Birds know naturally to build complex nests rapidly that even humans cannot easily do.

Sea turtles migrating thousands of kilometers to lay eggs at the same location they were born at is another example. Since this was a location of their own birth, the turtles would have had a natural inclination that it would be safe for them too. However, we know this is not the case as they have to run the gauntlet of birds and other fish waiting to eat them while they try to get back to the sea. And only a few make it from the many born. Or maybe it is something in the sand that drives them to this location, even with this danger for their young. Also, they apparently do not locate their bearings to come back later as they are running to the water as soon as they come out of the sand. Then there are other issues as they do not dig deeper in the sand but up to the surface and know the direction of the sea as soon as they come out of their shells.

In all these cases, it seems, their parents did not give them specific training to achieve this but somehow passed that information to their young at their birth. Most probably, the Creator would have programmed the parents' genes to this end. As for the birds, this may have been a gentle encouragement perhaps, or as the saying goes, a 'kick in the butt' to prompt them to try and start flying. This knowledge of how to fly would have been already inbuilt into their brains at birth. Otherwise, no matter how much kick in the butt it would be, the bird would never be able to fly. There are many such examples to justify this notion of having the newborn survival somehow being pre-programmed at birth.

This consequently tends to support the argument of an intelligent creator who created beings with inbuilt knowledge for survival. Other than this, there is no proof of the existence of such a creator than supposedly stated by few people who were selected to speak on behalf of this creator among the many billions of human beings who have been in existence up to this time.

Of course, who put the programming in the Creator to create all this? If this is the case, then most certainly, the only argument for the justification of this theory is that we will know all of this only after our death. However, not one of the billions of populations mentioned has come back from death to prove this. Then, we hear of near-death experiences of some to this effect. Unfortunately, they all speak of the Creator they met in relation to their own prior belief, leaving doubts of the reality of what they experienced.

The other school of thought, which we call science, says this is due to a big bang or big bang theory. Simply put, it was a highly unimaginable dense and hot quantity of what we call energy as small as a teaspoon that, under unimaginable compression, exploded and expanded as pure energy in the form of waves. This is called the 'wave theory.' By virtue of expansion and consequent cooling, this energy in waveform condensed to form hard or physical entities or subatomic particles called electrons, protons, and neutrons with perhaps other particles that were exact opposite in nature, which scientists call the antimatter. Examples would be positron for the electron etc. Interestingly, scientists by experiment have shown that when two such particles collide, they annihilate themselves to create pure energy, lending credence to this theory. In this universe, fortunately, we seem to have an abundance of electrons, protons, and neutrons than the existence of the antimatter particles. Maybe they are in another universe. Otherwise, matter, as we know, will not be able to exist, as we know that matter and antimatter cannot exist together.

The electrons, protons, and neutrons by themselves make what scientists call atoms. All these atoms have a hard center area made of protons and neutrons packed together with the electrons flying around. The number of protons in the center defines what type of element it is, such as carbon, nickel, iron, oxygen, or nitrogen in their pure form. These atoms, in turn, join with other atoms of the same type or others in different configurations to make matter or the hard substances we feel or see. As an example, a single iron atom linking with many other iron atoms form large iron particles. At the same time, a single iron atom will join with several oxygen atoms to form what we call Ferrous Oxide or rust. This different matter then coagulates to form larger masses, which manifest a phenomenon called heat and gravity. Gravity attracts other masses and creates planets, stars, etc., which in turn made our solar system. Many of these billions of solar systems make galaxies, and many billions of galaxies make what we do not know. Maybe a different universe?

So, the question now is, is there any truth behind this theory? Alternatively, scientists have discovered by experiments the configuration of atoms. They have even split the atoms into the said electrons, protons, and neutrons. Now, how the said energy made these subatomic particles is a question to raise. Considering this, we will now look at what is happening in the sun, which gives us heat and light. For this, the sun does sustain nuclear explosions by converting hydrogen gas into helium gas through a process called 'Nuclear Fusion.'

The process of this is that two hydrogen atoms fuse together to make a helium atom, which is less in mass than the initial two hydrogen atoms. As per scientists, matter cannot be destroyed, and the now missing mass is converted to energy in the form of sound, heat, and light that we know of on Earth.

In a similar manner, in a nuclear explosion called nuclear fission, a very heavy atom of elements called Uranium or Plutonium is made unstable, and this causes it to split into other atoms, which are less in total mass than the original heavy atom. The result of this is heat, light, and sound in waveforms. Effect of this we know from the Hiroshima atomic bomb devastation and, of course, the peaceful use of nuclear energy, where such heat is harvested as steam to drive turbines to generate electricity.

Now, we have seen a mass converted to energy in a waveform. This gives credence to the possibility of the opposite effect of energy in waveform manifesting as mass, as stated above. On the negative side of this theory, there is no explanation as to how this initial teaspoon of energy came into existence, creating the 'Big Bang.'

The irony is that it is irrelevant how the teaspoon of energy became a mass or who created the Creator as we are now experiencing economic pain and suffering during this short time here on Earth and need a remedy for this now and not in the next life. Another matter that is also of certainty is the impermanence of all living things and even things made from hard substances, such as the sun, moon, planets, or galaxies. They, too, are changing their state all the time and are in an unimaginable state of flux, exploding and then reforming in front of our own eyes as observed through powerful telescopes such as the Hubble.

Now, let's discuss the obvious question of how humans appeared or where they came from. Darwin's theory of evolution says that man evolved from a monkey to an ape and then to man. This was perhaps due to apes, while trying to adapt to the changes in the environment for survival, evolved into a man. He tried to prove this by making a comparison of the skull and showing how they altered from one to another with time and possible changes to the environment they lived in. Here we are not questioning as to where the monkeys came from, but an alternative school of thought says they came from an animal form from the sea, which was the result of microscopic animals forming from the required chemicals of life from space rocks or meteorites. This may have even been created by God or came from another planet.

To this end, we can experience evolution happening in this life by seeing our own skin, for example, changing to form a protective hard skin due to continuous rubbing at the same location. This is also the basis of evolution, adapting to the environment for survival, as explained by Darwin. As Earth would have done during its birth, we now can create the basic life builder, an amino acid known as DNA or Deoxyribonucleic Acid strands, the foundation of all life on Earth, under laboratory conditions as was done by Nobel Prize-winning scientist 'Arthur Kornberg' in 1959.

This was supposed to have been like the conditions Earth was experiencing during its formation.

The difference in the DNA of chimps and humans is only supposed to be approximately 1.2%. This means small changes in our DNA have made significant manifestations of highly intelligent dexterous humans going to space and somewhat intelligent chimps still living in trees. We also know there is only a small difference, approximately 0.1%, in the DNA of ordinary humans that created some great scientists and entrepreneurs vs. the dumbest we have on this earth. The point here is that we see small changes in DNA have made great humans from chimps.

By synthesizing the DNA in a lab, it also has been proven that the environment could affect changes to DNA. Also, the effect of radiation can also result in mutations in living things. An example of this is the Chernobyl nuclear disaster area, where animal and human mutations have been witnessed in the form of children born with more than two limbs and even two heads. This gives credence to the fact, as said before, that Darwin's theory of evolution is a strong possibility proving the effect of environment on the DNA.

On the other hand, we cannot explain why all living beings have the desire to propagate their species. Alternatively, how the first living being came into existence and immediately had the desire and the sexual organs in the correct anatomic configuration to propagate one's species with an opposite partner with the matching organs is a thought to ponder over indeed.

Hence the great question is, 'what came first? The chicken or the egg?' However, it can somewhat be explained that initial life came from unisex species, such as amoeba, which just splits itself for reproduction, or maybe even bacteria that split for propagation. Then one would wonder whether it had a sexual desire to split or if nature propelled it to split as fruits ripen on their own due to chemical reaction that takes place within them at the correct time of the season for their propagation—hence continuity of its species.

From studying many fossils of ancient humans and animals, it was concluded that man, animals, and plants have evolved with time. If our eyes do not lie to us, we know that our own manipulation of chromosomes, which are the building blocks of cells in our body at conception, can cause birth defects. This implies that it is not a creator but the properties of the chromosomes of DNA that make us what we are and all the other living beings.

If a creator has done this, this creation is expected to be foolproof and not have any loopholes, which now allow relatively unintelligent beings to mess with it or even fix the original screw-ups by this creator. As of now, scientists are on the verge of identifying possible birth defects of human embryos that may lead to diseases in the newborn and attempt to fix these prior to the birth of that child. Comparatively, say in this life, a first-grade student comes and fixes an error of a project developed by a Ph.D.

professor who is supposed to be the ultimate knowledge person on that subject.

Scientists have determined that environmental conditions also affect the DNA in embryos. This is observed by the deformities of humans and animals at birth and even plants near the Chernobyl nuclear disaster due to atomic radiation, as mentioned before. Notwithstanding this, scientists have subjected experimental animals to radiation and observed birth defects in their offspring, not to mention the animal itself getting diseases, such as cancer. This basically proves that the abnormal changes to the functioning of the cells can be caused by external events, the foundation of life. What this says is that evolution is possibly a fact, as environmental or chemical effects on the initial conceived embryo DNA could have caused changes to the DNA giving birth to new species. They would have then superseded the existing if they were more suitable to the environment for survival. This would not happen if humans were designed by a creator who is an all-encompassing entity, created in his own image as an expected absolute pure design.

From this, we see that a newborn's physical condition could change. If a new being is better suited to the current changed environmental condition than its predecessors, its survival would be much higher than its existing species. An example would be if a new human is born with less perspiring skin in a hot environment where less water is available, this species' propagated trait would be dominant and could survive while its relatives may die due to lack of water and more loss of water from their bodies.

And at the same time, the newborn will pass this new trait genetically to others to be born. Alternatively, if the new birth were inferior to the existing, it would not have a chance to propagate and would be extinct. This is also a part of the theory of human evolution by Darwin, as mentioned before. Similarly, if a tiger can sense its prey at a distance due to its superior eyesight and has higher speed, this tiger would have a better chance of survival than the other tigers at a time when the abundance of prey is no longer.

Now, in my opinion, birth is the first division of the combined DNA of the parents, which lays the footprint of what is to be born. It is also my belief that the initiation of electrical energy flow from the split of the first male and female combined cell is the beginning of the foundation of life. A question may be asked as to why the beginning of life cannot be at the time of the union of the male and female chromosomes or the first combined cell. The answer to the question, in my opinion, is that it requires some sort of external initiation to make the initial cell split happen. As for the physical form of the newborn, it will be dictated by the combined chromosomes or DNA but not the traits of the newborn.

Human skills for things, such as handicrafts, or their traits, such as a quick temper, are not derived from the physical form and is not even possible to gain from something in the chromosomes or

DNA. To me, this is most unlikely and must be something external coming into the conceived entity. If this is not the case, how does a toad or newborn frog know how to swim, a honeybee know how to suck honey from flowers, and a weaverbird know how to weave a complex nest that even we cannot easily do as they are not trained to do this when they are young? If we assume this, too, comes from information embedded in the chromosomes as an electrical or another type of signal, how can the newborn have different skills than the parents most of the time? Or are the survival skills alone coded in the chromosomes as electrical signals?

For example, the father may be good at electrical work but not in accounts. The mother may be good at needlework but not skilled in accounts, and neither the son nor the daughter may be good at electrical work or needlework but skilled in accounts. As said before, only the survival skills are inherited this way via information stored in the chromosomes. There may be some traits that are unique to one and not brought to this life from the traits of the parents, which means not from anything that is embedded in the chromosomes of the fertilized mother's embryo. This is known by some as **Karma** or, for some, God's will. However, this may come from something called the dark matter or dark energy surrounding us in the universe, as scientists now say, which we cannot see or feel or something that is there, and we have no idea about it currently. Conversely, do we impart something to the dark matter or dark energy when we think or do things strong enough to carry it to our next life if we believe in rebirth? What we can merely say is that there is something we bring forward to this life that makes each of us have different traits, even if we are twins, triplets, or quadruplets.

Well, what does all this have to do with the economy? As for humans, this, to some extent, defines the capability of the newborn to be an entrepreneur who will make financial opportunities happen even from nothing. As an example, the ability to take an unusual rock formation at some remote place and give it a fancy name and then put up gift shops, restaurants, children's parks, etc., around it and get people to come to visit this location and spend their money. This also creates an opportunity for others in the surrounding area to earn a living with new motels, gas stations, or supermarkets to cater to the visitors to this site.

Does this mean that people like Steve Jobs, Henry Ford, and Howard Hughes will be reborn with the same traits in the next life? That we do not know, but what we do know is, such persons with such traits may surely be born all the time among the many millions of newborns every day. This would affect the economic conditions of the environment they live in if they are allowed to flourish in the society they are born in, which means if such a person is born to a Communist country or to a poor family in a Capitalist society, the possibility of this person developing entrepreneurship capabilities to affect that society's economy positively would be severely limited.

The bottom line is that evolution creates human progress from primates to a current highly complex society that needs entrepreneurs to sustain and grow the economy in order for all its people to have a sustained opportunity to make money to live their lives.

Chapter 2: Human Birth

When a human is born, he or she is automatically subject to economic conditions faced by the parents. Meaning, the parents may not have enough money to buy milk for the child. The child may not have a comfortable bed to sleep on etc. After all, at birth, he or she has no knowledge of, neither direction nor control of what its future is going to be. For a fortunate few, the birth would be a wanted one. It would be well-planned, well-fed from the mother's womb, and born to a socially acceptable environment to legally wed parents. And if you are further lucky in an economic sense, as a very few would have its privileges already in place, you would inherit a financial fortune and would not have to undergo the hardship of life. For some, it would be an incident to avoid at all costs if it was a possibility. If it's not, their life would be an example of misery, pain, and suffering, in general, and for some who are further unfortunate, there would be utterly bitter experiences, such as loss of parents at birth, deformity, non-ending diseases, hunger, or premature death. For the rest, somewhere in between.

However, this does not mean that a child born under the worst deprivation cannot live in peace and contentment. This is achieved by understanding one's own desires and not being affected by things such as lust, greed, and hate, which is, of course, easier said than done. One must also not be affected even when all the possible misfortune comes in their way. Now, we would look at a possible example to this end. A promising young dancer loses a leg by amputation due to cancer. Now, if this person can fully understand and accept what has happened without remorse and be happy that his or her life has been spared, he or she may even become a famous rich politician with one leg. People will even admire his or her courage.

This denotes one's true understanding of the surroundings and not the conditions at birth or an unfortunate incident in life that would ultimately lead to a productive and happy life in this world. On the other hand, even the luckiest person, as per our economic definition, may take their own life due to a loss of purpose even though they have the ability to get anything at whim to satisfy their economic desires but are unable to satisfy their psychological or mental needs. To this end in history, we have seen supposed-to-be-heirs to vast fortunes ending up being murderers or even drug addicts. In all honesty, they seem to be looking for that elusive happiness even by mental hallucination.

Others in a similar situation with all the wealth will thrive for recognition from society. Some may genuinely be interested in the betterment of humans, animals, or the environment and get involved in charity, social services, or humanitarian services to find that purpose in life and make good use of their wealth.

Then, there would also be that remnant with or without wealth who would live a contented life of satisfaction and bliss by dedicating one's life not only to oneself but also to all living beings. Therefore, it should be noted that we did not mention happiness but bliss, as happiness is momentary, but bliss is more deep-rooted and lingering. This bliss brings deeper contentment, which we all directly or indirectly strive to achieve in this life one way or the other.

Hence, the more one develops their mind by focusing on the reality of things around them by using the power of reasoning, the more likely it is for them to understand the true nature of life and, in the end, leading to salvation from pain and suffering. This, of course, is irrespective of whatever social status, riches, or fame already achieved. Though we all have this unidentified inner capacity to blossom with a true understanding of our nature by our power of reasoning, most of us will not achieve it. Unfortunately, this is due to distractions and other forces in life, which constantly affect us, such as hunger, sickness, the need to make a living, etc. which mostly consume all our time.

As such, it would be difficult to focus by looking at our own conduct and surrounding rationally. In this situation, the author of this book sincerely hopes his writing would provide an impetus to kindle that thought process in our own mind in time to initiate and sustain a spark of that curiosity. At the very least, to emulate another human being who has already developed such capability in order to spark that interest.

There is much debate as to what stage constitutes the birth of a child – the time a child is born into this world from the mother's womb or the time of conception. The last option seems more logical of the two. However, if you take single-cell animals, there is no joining of two chromosomes but the splitting of its own chromosomes or DNA. Hence, it is the opinion of the writer that birth is the first initiation of communication in the DNA strands to cause this split to make a new cell or new animal. In superior animals, this, of course, is the initiation of communication for the splitting of the DNA in the embryo containing the DNA of both the male and female.

The characteristics of some of those born may contribute to the economy positively by uplifting the living conditions of many others, such as current and past entrepreneurs like Henry Ford, Howard Hughes, Bill Gates, Elon Musk, and Steve Jobs, to name a few. Similarly, people or companies that raise prices while still making good profits because they can, as some drug companies do, contribute negatively to the economy and are referred to as Black Marketers. Hence, it is evident the character an individual brings to this world at birth may be for good or evil to the economy of the masses.

On the other hand, even those black marketers were helped by great scientists, such as Benjamin Franklin, who discovered electricity; Thomas Edison, who designed the electric bulb; Nikola Tesla, who founded the Electrical AC Generation; and Alexander

Fleming, who discovered penicillin, etc. Without these discoveries, the black marketers would not have been able to develop their products or services and even sometimes live. The point here is that some black marketers have no gratitude to the extent of fleecing consumers if they can if the opportunity arises—even them already benefitting from the selflessness of the others.

However, we will not be discussing who discovered the 'wheel,' the greatest invention, which is significant to the economy, as we do not know this information. The wheel has facilitated human birth by providing a method for travel to hospitals for pregnant mothers, to say the least, without which some of us may not be here now.

Also, there is another type of scientist called Theoretical or Astrophysicists, which include notable names, such as Albert Einstein or late Stephen Hawkings, whose postulations do not immediately contribute to the economy, but in time guide other scientists with discoveries to benefit the economy of the masses.

However, when the theories of theoretical physicists sometimes contribute to the economy, the effect is always profound. For instance, Einstein's equation of $E=m(c*c)$ gave rise to the development of the atomic bomb many years later, ending the disastrous World War II. At the same time, it helped develop nuclear energy by providing electrical energy for environmentally friendly industrial development, which is, of course, debatable because the nuclear waste it generates is not easily disposable and very hazardous to human health. Then, there is the issue of nuclear bombs, which some argue has kept peace in the world, contributing to the substance of the economy of the world. And when nuclear energy via fission is practical, it would provide unlimited pollution-free energy for humanity's economic progress, especially for the industrialized countries. By the same token, the nuclear bomb will wipe out all the economics of the world with its inhabitants if it ever happens.

Finally, we have seen that an inherent capability of a human may dictate what our economy would be by virtue of traits they bring to this world at birth. This, in turn, may or may not be facilitated by the environment they are born into when blossomed or inhibited into maturity.

Chapter 3: Mind and Senses

If we have no mind for dissemination of information and a sense for gathering information, we will not survive. In this scenario, there would be no economy as we may not be born in the first place, or even if we are born, we will die of starvation as we will not be able to feed ourselves by not knowing how to grow food etc. However, survival may be possible by absorbing nourishing ingredients directly from air automatically and synthesizing them as required within our body as plants do. Unfortunately, we are not biologically made for this.

Earlier, we looked at the very moment when a birth or life is supposed to begin. Life to us means the one born would have some or many means for power for decision-making. We identify plants as living beings even if they do not make decisions but chemically respond to the environment, even though some think they sense danger and communicate among themselves to this end. Meaning they have physical senses we cannot see or detect.

As for this book, they are not living beings in the sense of animals and humans. This means, from the animal kingdom to humans, they have sensory organs, such as eyes, ears, nose, etc., for touch, sound, sight, taste, and a brain to disseminate the information coming from them. With humans, unlike animals, our decision-making seems somewhat strongly based on our past life happenings or traits brought forward to this life in us, apart from the sensory inputs from the above sensory organs. This does not mean to say that all the dogs in a litter are identical in their traits as they all bark the same or show the same lovingness, which is not the case. However, the development of their mind is constrained or enhanced to this end by their physical form. Enhanced like humans due to the dexterity of the limbs, ability to form complex sounds or make a speech, etc. Most of all, based on its sensory inputs, humans can make complex rational decisions based on past stored knowledge very much more than any animal we know of.

In all, each one of us born into this world tends to differ in one's actions, temperaments, capabilities, such as leadership skills and entrepreneurship skills, etc. These are then tempered by what we call our upbringing, including religion, caste, creed, parental affluence, and status in society. In the end, such tempered traits or capabilities become resident in oneself. We understand this as our minds enable us to develop further with the help of the inputs from education as we grow.

There are many theories as to how a human being and his mind came into existence. However, prior to understanding this aspect, it is my view that we first need to know what our senses are saying is true or not. Are they true all the time or only sometimes?

Consider magic. From this, we know that our senses do not tell us the truth all the time. One may argue that if this is the case, how could we do things, such as fly a plane or drive a car, for this requires all our senses to be focused and be validated by the changes in the surroundings? The answer to this question lies in the reasoning power of our minds. It helps us know when we are fooled by our senses by understanding the true nature of our surroundings as we experience things. So how does the mind do this? It does so by experience or knowledge it has gathered previously. For example, if one puts a stick into a glass of water and tells another that the water has bent the stick, our education tells us that this is not true, and it is an optical phenomenon. If we did not know this by experience or had not been told by someone else, we would believe that the water has bent the stick.

This brings to light the part of our minds that helps in distinguishing fact from fiction, which now is mainly based on our education or through experience passed on from generation to generation. This is possible by increasing our in-depth knowledge and content being validated by many peers or, most importantly, having the ability to achieve the same end results by the same initiating conditions every time. This is called **Science**. A simple example would be not to light a match at a gas station. Though we are not going to light a match at a gas station to find out what happens, being told by others with experience or information to this effect substantiated by our own mind, we rationalize that gas and fire do not go together as it causes an explosion.

Therefore, whatever we discuss below, it is important to be positive about what we believe to be true. One way for this is to know that we could achieve the same results by repeating the same initial conditions every time. However, going back to the example of the pencil in the glass bending, this cannot be the basis to determine something to be true or false all the time.

An interesting situation comes to my mind in this regard. I used to wear spectacles in my teenage. Due to the advent of contact lenses, I tried them. Suddenly all the objects I saw were bigger in size than before. So, I took a measuring tape and measured an object wearing my spectacles and then the contact lenses. To my surprise, the measurement was the same. Then, I realized the tape too was bigger when I used the contact lenses, giving me the same result. Now that I know the eye is filled with fluid, how does this affect the reality of what I perceive to exist around me in conjunction with what the water does to the pencil?

Hence, the key to understanding the reality of our world would be an educated mind or having an open mind to absorb and disseminate information wherever it comes from. Dissemination should be done with our own reasoning and not being dogmatic by virtue of birth or through information passed down by someone else without proof. However, one may ask, if this is the case, how we could progress in life if not by learning from what others have told us through what we call education.

For this, we need to look at our minds. Yet, where is this mind? We know where our senses are when we block it, and we feel the sense of simulation disappearing. An example would be if we closed our eyes, we would lose our vision. The most popular belief is that the mind resides in the brain, and in some instances where half of the brain has been removed by a 'hemispherectomy,' the mind tends to remain intact other than the loss of motor skills, such as moving limbs or speech. One thing to be noted is that the mind I am referring to here is not the part of the brain that controls our speech, movement, etc. but the mind that gives us the power of reasoning.

One may argue that the mind is like a central processor unit or the CPU or the Central Processing Unit of a computer. However, the computer does not make decisions but follows the instructions given to it and hence is dumb as hell. These instructions come in the form of what we call the user program stored in the computer memory by the user. This effectively tells the computer to do this or that, if it gets this input etc. But what initiates this action of the computer? This is the clock of the computer, which uses the naturally occurring oscillations of a crystal to generate a fixed frequency of electrical pulses of a fixed duration.

Therefore, when the computer is powered, it applies electricity to the electronic circuits, which uses the crystal's natural vibration to generate a regulated electrical pulse train that gives 'life' to the computer. These pulses drive the activity of the computer as per the instructions or program built into it. What then is its relationship to the human mind? Even if the five senses, which are sight, touch, hearing, taste, and smell, provide data to the brain, there must be a mechanism that initiates the selectively processing of information coming from the said sensory organs. Not only to store them but also to be able to recover this information when required. 'When required' is an important clue here. For humans, this is our preprogrammed mind, which comes with birth and is always looking at the sensory inputs from the ear, eye, nose, etc., for any signals to process as per instructions built into our brains from somewhere we do not know of.

Now, if we consider a newborn baby, as soon as they open their eyes, a picture of what they see is available to the brain because the nerves react to the light falling on the eye. This happens due to a chemical process that takes place in the retina of the eye. This information is then automatically transmitted to the brain. But now, something should tell the brain to capture this information and store it after disseminating the information as useful or not. In the reverse form, the mind detects the baby to be hungry and sends a command to the mouth and nose to smell and find food or suckle the mother even if the baby has not opened the eyes yet. The baby would, in turn, use the information stored in the brain to detect the mothers' nipples to this end, maybe by a particular smell or taste. Meaning, even if a feeder bottle is kept nearby, it would try suckling the mother as the baby knows what it requires to survive its hunger in the first instance. This proves the baby has preprogrammed information in its brain.

When a living being is born, critical information is pre-stored as data and transferred to its embryo for its survival. This is the same as pre-stored information in the ROM (read-only memory) of a computer being transferred to the RAM (read and write memory) of a computer when a computer is booted up or powered. How this information gets there in the human or animal world is another issue, as touched on before. The important thing is that this sets the foundation for human beings to become great economic visionaries like Henry Ford, Bill Gates, Howard Hughes, Steve Jobs, or the great scientific minds, such as Marconi, Mari Quire, or Einstein, and many others who have taken the quality of human existence to a higher level by providing opportunities for human economic sustainability. This is done via what we call jobs for the masses, with their end vision of making sure that the scientific knowledge is freely available to the masses to develop new products or create new products for better economic sustenance and, as said before, even to the black marketers.

Now, does this have a connection to the parent's background? No. This is because most newborns' parents have not been economic visionaries or scientific minds themselves, according to my knowledge. Therefore, it seems to suggest that this ROM data or the initial information to the living embryos did not come from the parents. Most likely, it came from something outside the embryos, with something in the embryo selectively facilitating its entry. To this end, I wonder whether any scientist has tried to crossbreed a pig and a tiger or a carnivore and an herbivore to see what comes out of it if it is successful. This can shed light on the qualities this new animal would be having, such as eating meat or rotten food. Or crossbreed two birds who build different types of nests and see what type of nest the crossbreed bird would make.

Furthermore, we can see if any external energy gets into the embryo at conception by trying to place the parents, such as a cock and a hen, inside a magmatic cocoon field to make chicks if possible. This is in the expectation that the magnetic field can interact with whatever is supposed to come to the embryo from the outside.

However, the enclosed magnetic field may not have any effect on whatever is expected to come from outside to the embryo. However, if it happens, meaning the eggs will not hatch or even if there are no eggs being laid or even the hatchlings get deformed, it would tend to prove that something does come to the embryo from outside which interacts with electromagnetic energy, or at the least would provide further impetus for further research to this end.

It is also interesting to note, as an example, how a bird knows to make a particular type of nest specific to its kind. This information cannot come from the previous birth unless one believes that when a particular bird dies, it would always be born as the same type of bird, where the imprint of such critical data for survival was passed down from the soul of the dead bird to the newborn by some mechanism.

To me, the rationale for this lies in the possibility of such information becoming imprinted in the DNA of every sperm and ovary cell of the animal, defining what that animal is to be born as. When a particular animal is born, this information becomes part of the newborn. Now, the important correlation of this to the economy is when some information for survival is generic by virtue of birth, while some mechanisms or traits are derived from the previous birth somehow.

In effect, the human's survival and its economic wellbeing depend on the personality traits of the newborn and its ability to survive at birth by knowing how to suckle the mother or a feeding bottle for food. Furthermore, carrying on that entrepreneurship, scientific, or economic skills from one's past life to this birth contributes to the advancement of the economy he or she is born into. So, there must have been something in our minds or brain that updates the existing knowledge with additional knowledge gained in this life and pass it to the next birth as artificial intelligence or AI as known in the computer world. Or is it possible that, say, for example, when a human dies and is born as a monkey, the traits this human has developed get to the monkey too but are not able to manifest due to its monkey form? This seems to fit with the concept of karma, which we will look at in more detail later.

Or all this may be possible because we have learned to write and store our gained knowledge, which could be used by the next generation as the starting point to extend their knowledge further and upgrade these writings and pass it on to the next generation again. This way, it helps to continuously upgrade our civilization and economy.

Consequent to the initial survival and knowledge coming from birth, the archeological information has shown beyond any doubt that humans have evolved from a primitive species living in caves to the current mansions equipped with all the modern conveniences, such as electronic gadgets, to make life easier. All the different medicines, development of machinery, space exploration, etc., are proofs that we are still evolving. Substantiating this is the information that in some nations, people are now taller due to eating McDonald's.

With all this complexity of possibilities, the next point here is to understand that, though we are now communicating in sophisticated languages and building machinery for our comfort and explore space, etc., did we come to this point suddenly, or through a civilized beginning as defined at the beginning of this book? In fact, even now, our conduct can be savage like an animal. We show this side of human behavior by killing each other in wars and commit atrocities, such as butchering humans by cutting arms, legs, etc. This is done without any mercy in order to protect our resources when needed or even just to show loyalty to one's perceived god or country.

As ordinary people like farmers, schoolteachers, or medics, we would never even comprehend that we can be driven to such a state, but during wars, we do. Irrespective of wars, even in our normal day-to-day life, we do bad things for selfish reasons. This tells us that our origin would have probably been savage but has consequently been civilized. As such, humans did not suddenly manifest as civilized humans to maintain a coherent society for economic sustenance but evolved due to the need to survive as a group or society.

We have spent much time understanding the characteristics of the mind of a newborn and what they would become and how they would affect our economy later. However, now the question is, what do the mind and sense have to do with the economy? The obvious answer, in part, is the capability of the mind that enabled a person to dream up a business and take it from its infancy to a blooming conglomerate that provides opportunities to the masses to make money for its survival. The mind had the ability to convince the consumer to part with their money to enjoy products or services for either a temporary purpose, such as eating a bar of chocolate, or long-term purposes, such as buying a car. This also includes the vision and the ability to make such products.

Is this ability the trait which initially a newborn gets at birth, as per what we discussed earlier? These traits are enhanced with time during each birth cycle, possibly by the effects of what is known as **Karma** as mentioned before (which is supposed to follow us through each life) and further enhanced or retarded by his or her current birth condition or the environment that person is born into.

And now, has it created entrepreneurs, such as Steve Jobs from a Stone Age ape? We may never know. However, we have seen that our economy is dependent upon the ability of such people's minds, capabilities, and desires to create employment opportunities for others, directly or indirectly, in the backdrop of creating wealth for themselves, or for purely egoistic reasons, or for the sole benefit of humanity, or a combination of all these.

Chapter 4: Animal Kingdom

Do animals have an economy? In my opinion, it could be a yes and no, depending on how you look at what they face to survive. If their environment and climate are such that they have good availability of food, and they could survive without doing much other than walking to it or chasing it, killing and eating the same, then it is a 'no,' as there is nothing they need to do to survive. Also, no, because they are unable to alter the availability of the food supply, such as genetically modifying food for higher production, selection, or crossbreeding to suit harsh environmental conditions as humans do. Thus, they depend on raw resources, such as fruits, meat, etc., as nature provides for them to ensures their survival, as stated earlier. Humans, on the other hand, can make drinking water from seawater when water is scarce or grow food in greenhouses when the climate is harsh. This permits the survival of the species when such needs become critical and economically viable.

The question we like to ask now is whether the animals experience economic situations that humans experience. The answer to this would be 'Yes' but not to the extent of humans. For example, we know animals guard their territory. This is because they protect their resources for themselves or for their group. These resources would be for food or safety. However, luckily for them, they do not have to worry about clothing, medicine, or money.

Sadly, for them, they are very dependent on the weather conditions to ensure they have sufficient food available to survive. Some animals, instead of guarding their territory all the time for their resources, migrate to other locations during seasons to ensure the availability of food and shelter. Therefore, in the animal world, we see that their economy is all about the availability of food, shelter, and safety. Thus, when animals live in a land with plenty to eat and are safe, their economy is 100%. Nevertheless, for humans, even if they have plenty to eat without working for it and their living conditions are safe, their economy cannot be considered 100%, as they need additional things, such as medication for sicknesses or, more importantly, they need luxuries, such as cars, jewelry, and travel to satisfy their ego.

Chapter 5: The Universe or Space

What does the universe have to do with our economy? What is the connection between the two? Our economy needs raw materials to produce all sorts of stuff, ranging from TVs, computers, mobile phones to medical equipment. Some of these raw materials are not abundant on Earth or easily accessible. Hence, they are known as rare earth materials. Now, imagine us suddenly finding out that these elements are not available. Millions of people worldwide will become unemployed because some pieces of equipment needing these rare materials can no longer be manufactured.

This will suddenly reduce revenue to the government but would see a hike in expenditure to care for the newly unemployed. Then they will have to provide unemployment benefits, such as food stamps or other free benefits, or create more government jobs. This will increase the government expenditure. All these actions by the government would be to prevent possible riots by such unemployed masses seeking a change of government as they always blame the government for their current situation when things of this nature happen, whether it is justified or not.

Hence, the government, with selected individuals controlling the economy, whom the people may have elected or not, would want to retain their livelihood and avoid this situation. Therefore, to cover the increased expenditure, the government will impose an increased percentage of taxes on the working people and businesses. The government may even print more money to cover the additional expenditure.

If we had a balanced economy, almost everyone would have a meaningful livelihood, with the government revenue from taxes being sufficient to cover the government expenditure. Now, imagine the repercussions if there is a reduction in oil and gas as well as rare earth material, now widely used in electronic items and mobile phones, etc. This may be due to using all the rare earth materials we are left with or not doing new explorations to find new sources. Even the current solar and wind energy capture seems to have maxed out. As for solar and wind energy, it requires a large mass of batteries, which would not be available now due to the lack of said mineral resources to manufacture them. Also, in my opinion, capturing wind energy can cause drastic climatic changes as in my opinion, the flow of the wind is essential to maintain our climatic conditions. Not only this, the heat, which normally is absorbed by the ground, will now be reflected back to the air by all these vast arrays of solar panels heating the air and disturbing its flow patterns. This may, in turn, contribute to climate change. This is like, as the saying goes, when you disturb nature, it has a way of hitting you back.

Knowing this situation is emerging, we start building and sending manned or robotic flights to other planets in outer space or even to certain asteroids to get these minerals or to harvest these to sustain our economy. This results in more economic activity on Earth, like building these required space vehicles, setting up local infrastructure, and doing more research and development or R&D to upgrade these spaceships, etc. These expeditions may even find an abundance of energy resources that are currently unknown and can be substituted for oil and gas to serve our energy needs on Earth or may be even pure water to supplement what we are polluting on Earth.

Alternatively, placing large solar panels in deep outer space, positioned to capture sun energy around the clock and use reflectors to reflect it to different locations on Earth as microwaves 24/7, negates the use of large batteries to store power as with current solar panels used on Earth, especially for night use when there is no sunlight. This would require new industries to build and maintain these solar arrays and reflectors, fleets of rockets for their transport to space to installation and service, as well as to launch new space stations. There will also be a need for large numbers of people to control and manage these activities. Another positive effect of such reflectors would be their ability to be placed in Earth's orbit in such a way that it would not interfere with the sunlight falling onto Earth.

Furthermore, countries would compete to make better models of these flying machines to do this work more efficiently. This would eventually create more work opportunities for the masses. The production would be competitive in the market to do this as cost-effectively as possible, contributing to sustenance or growth of the economy of those countries. In the event Earth is the only planet in this universe, this could, of course, not be applicable, as we would not be able to find these resources by exploring other planets but only asteroids. However, we now know there are thousands of other planets called Exoplanets; some are even similar to our planet, meaning their large physical bodies go around stars in ours as well as other galaxies.

As an example, consider how many people NASA of the USA currently employs? Thousands. They send rockets to space to explore outer space. For a long time, we knew Earth rotates at a specific speed. By virtue of Earth's rotation speed, they could place satellites in specific locations in space whose speed could match the rotation speed of Earth. Hence, to an observer on Earth, the satellite would look as if it remains stationary. This was first postulated by the world-renowned writer Arthur C. Clark. This allowed the bouncing of radio signals off these satellites so that the signal could be sent to another fixed location on Earth far away from the line of sight. Line of sight means the distance we can see from our naked eye, which is approximately 7 miles. This possibility was important since now people could communicate with others all over the world instantly via these satellites interspersed in space.

This method of communication gave rise to many industries to expedite trade between the countries of the world, making our world a 'small world' as the saying goes. As a result, economies expanded significantly. For example, now, a trader in the US could instantly order shoes from China without having to send a letter by regular post, which would have taken days to reach the supplier in China. Hence, this would increase sales by meeting customer demands faster.

By the development of the GPS (using signals from such three geo-stationery satellites to compute a location on Earth) signals, now we can navigate around the globe by knowing exactly where we are on Earth's surface all the time. By virtue of all these capabilities, we now have industries employing millions of people in the communication industry.

The point here is, due to our ability to go to space, which I believe was achieved due to our human curiosity, we have now given rise to many industries providing millions of people the opportunity to earn a living or to live in a better economic environment. Therefore, we see that our space activity has inadvertently created many opportunities for the masses of many countries and has improved their economies.

Imagine that we have a signal from a spacecraft that aliens are on their way to Earth. Suddenly, people would spend their money in droves to store all sorts of items as food, water, firearms, etc., increasing the production of these items. Increased production demands create a need for more labor, even temporarily. Subsequently, if the aliens do not come and the buyers are unable to consume the food, even kept refrigerated, the food would go to waste. The net effect would be that all the money has now gone to the economy to benefit others.

Another example would be, due to the fear of an asteroid strike on Earth, NASA is spending colossal amounts of money to pay scientists to make rockets to hit and divert the incoming asteroid or find other means to destroy it. Space X and few other companies are also spending millions of dollars currently to take humans to Mars and colonize it in the event of such a catastrophe happening, creating jobs for the masses. This also contributes to the world's economic activity via salaries to the employees, materials for building the infrastructure on Mars, and for building human habitats, required rockets, and its support facilities. If these companies succeed at sending humans to Mars, the economic activity that would be created on Earth by making all these maintaining equipment needed, transporting it to Mars and maybe beyond, would be colossal. Notwithstanding this, the returning rockets from Mars may bring new materials not found on Earth to make new products on Earth, facilitating more economic uptick on Earth.

In all this, what we see is that space or the universe has given us an opportunity to increase our economic activity by virtue of using the human curiosity of the unknown. In fact, space or the universe will be our opportunity for continuous creation of economic activity on Earth in the time to come.

Chapter 6: Family & Society

Let us first describe what we mean by **Family** here. A family is a unit comprising a man, a woman, and children born to them. The societies they live in consider a family to be ideal if it consists of legally married parents who are responsible for each other as per an acknowledgment certificate, commonly referred to as the marriage certificate, issued to them by the same societies.

Currently, however, this definition has become clouded in some countries. The important thing worth noticing is, a family is a group of co-existing adults and children. This highlights the legal responsibility of the parents or adults of the said family unit to sustain their offspring or adopted children and ensure they become productive citizens of society. To this end, the government has enacted laws to punish parents who do not meet this responsibility by fining or even jailing parents who do not send their children to school for education. Such government wants to ensure such a family does not become a burden or liability to the economy but a productive economic unit.

In effect, the family is an economically stable consuming unit of the resources around us, generating a market for the products of other people. As an example, they would all have a good breakfast, consuming maybe cereal, milk, butter, bread, etc., as the parents must ensure the children get a good meal in the morning. If this were only a loose setup of some children and adults, some would probably even skip breakfast and eat only when hungry—as a result, creating less demand for the resources, unlike a family unit. Hence, a family is a productive unit of society for its economic development.

Now, the meaning of the word 'productive' here is twofold – a consumption unit and a unit to develop technology for new products. In this regard, the consumption unit or the consumer would want more products that are efficient and hence cost-effective as well as convenient to use. Society would want to save on limited natural resources. Of course, the government tries to ensure the former by providing free schooling to children in most countries, at least to a certain level, so they would become educated to this end. In the US, the school fees are paid by taxes collected from the family units living in the area. In some countries, they are free for all the students, even at the university level. Also, some governments monitor the standard of teaching in schools to award scholarships or give grants to the poor who are gifted so that they may attend university. All this is done to ensure the children of a certain family unit become economically productive assets to the society instead of being a consuming unit living on welfare or other people's hard-earned money.

To understand the impact of a family or economy better, we would consider a scenario of each legal family unit having one child or no children at all. Even if we assume that these children will be productive members of society, in time, there will be a majority who would not be working as their parents retire. For example, as parents retire, fewer children would be entering the workforce, thus depriving the government of tax revenue. However, now the retiring people would be demanding more benefits from the government as Social Security, Medicare, and Medicate, etc. Hence, the government will have to print more money, leading to other economic situations, which we will discuss later in this book.

A family is the fundamental unit of a cohesive society, providing structure to an organization required to achieve a better economy. Consider the breadwinner of the family working hard to provide for his family. To this end, he or she tries to be productive (employee) and innovative at times (businessperson) to collect as much money as possible for the family. Having more children also means an increase in the consumption by the family, making a market for the producers to sell their products and siphon the parents' earned money back to the economy as wages to the producers' workers, etc. When educated children become working members of families, they would provide more tax revenue to the government, facilitating the government to pay social benefits to the retired people.

However, if the number of children in society increases too much (more children in families), a negative effect on the economy would occur. This means the natural resources available for the sustenance of society would not be sufficient. For example, consider that the food production of a country is stable with all available land being utilized for cultivation, but suddenly there are more people needing food. In this case, the government would have to import food from other countries. If this country does not produce what the other countries want, then it would face economic imbalances leading to riots and political turmoil as it would not have a product to sell to the country it is trying to import food from. However, if one or few of these new children get educated, say up to the Ph.D. level in plant biology and do research and come up with a new variety of high-yielding rice or wheat, the crisis may be mitigated temporally, giving the country time to address the situation by limiting the number of children a family can have.

In this regard, we should consider the situation of children coming out of wedlock and orphans without parents. Consequently, due to lack of attention and direction, they may lack the discipline to concentrate on their education during their upbringing. They would eventually be unemployed or would spend most of their life in prison. This would lead to a society with people who are consumers only but not educated enough to contribute to the economy progressively. Not to mention the contribution they could have made to the economy if properly educated and engaged in tasks, such as discovering high-yielding rice or wheat, as stated earlier, or other great inventions to uplift the economy.

Overall, it is noticeably clear that societies with better-organized family units with a balance of children in proportion to the resources of their society will contribute better to their economy.

Chapter 7: Education

Economists always say that education would promote greater economic development in a country. However, to me, this is both true and false. True in the sense that an average factory worker needs only a basic ability to read, write, and count in order to understand and fulfill their responsibilities. Gardeners, road sweepers, or garbage collectors do not need to have an education to that extent as compared to a clerical hand or a machine operator to do their work. On the other hand, an engineer needs a much higher level of education than them all to enable him to develop new machinery or maintain the existing by knowing advanced mathematics to do calculations, etc.

Scientists, on the other hand, need to master existing knowledge in their field as well as discover additional knowledge by research so the engineers can use the discoveries by scientists to develop new products. For example, a scientist in the field of physics may do research and develop a more powerful laser using his existing knowledge. The engineer may, in turn, use this and develop guidance or aiming systems to aim the laser accurately at an object far away, which could be mounted even on an unsteady platform in a harsh environment.

The bottom line is that education is of primary importance to take humans from the current level of economic growth to a higher level of economic activity. Today, we see mobile phones, smaller and faster computers, etc. in the market as a result of people of higher education, such as scientists and engineers, in the fields of electronics and communication doing research and development known as R&D. Now, in thinking that we need to increase such scientists and engineers so more such products can be made available, we may increase the education level of school dropouts from middle and high school by conducting additional classes so they could enter the universities.

If this happens, there would be lots of scientists and engineers and fewer factory workers, clerical staff, and a dearth of lower category employees, such as laborers. Not only this, some of these scientists and engineers may not be employable as there would be a saturation of the market for these more educated people, and they, in turn, will demand better jobs rather than engaging in lower category jobs at factories or as clerical workers.

This would create an imbalance in the economy as more people would be unemployed due to a lack of better jobs. Better education will lower the demand for doing what we call low-level work done by general laborers, cleaners, garbage collectors, packers, sorters, etc. In any economy, these positions are numerous compared to other higher-level jobs as clerks or machine workers. However, there is always an exception to this rule.

On the other hand, if we go back in history, we find that some of the most important factors affecting economic development have been people who were not highly educated scholars or having Ph.D.'s but people such as Howard Hughes, Bill Gates, or Steve Jobs. They did not do this through creating scientific inventions but by utilizing inventions by others for the development of products to be used by the masses, because they were visionaries, which is not a trait developed from acquiring education but an innate quality, as discussed before. For example, Bill Gates did not invent the computer. Other scientists did. However, Bill Gates made it user-friendly for the masses by developing Windows, which enabled ordinary people to use the computer by clicking on icons on the screen rather than typing complex commands.

Scientists with higher degrees, lesser degrees, or with no degrees discovered the Transistor, Electricity, X-Ray, Internet, the structure of DNA, etc. Entrepreneurs utilized these discoveries to make their products for use by the masses, benefiting the economy. Focused groups of scientists are also utilizing this knowledge to develop advanced things, such as nuclear and military weapons. Regrettably, in what we call developed countries, the impact of the industry that makes military products on their economies has been vast and makes up a major portion of the Gross Domestic Product (GDP) in the USA in particular. This, we will discuss later.

As discussed so far, we have seen the value of higher education in order to produce scientists, engineers, etc. The less educated are also needed for other work to keep the economy buzzing. But, at the minimum, we have seen the need for all to be educated with the skills of reading, writing, and some math so they could at least work with their money and carry on with their day-to-day activities, such as write a letter when needed or read a book, go to the market, and buy food and pay for it correctly, etc.

Education is not the only thing that could make people become entrepreneurs or visionaries. It only assists in grooming or polishing these inborn traits that they get from their parental genes or are inherited from their past life, as some call 'Karma,' which plays a great role or the greatest role for the development of the economy of a society.

Chapter 8: Science

It is interesting to understand some beliefs in the current era. Many people today and their predecessors before them have written textbooks specifically on subjects associated with what is taught in universities. These we take as the gospel truth today and believe that if we repeat what they said or observed, we will end up with or observe the same results as them. This is as they are supposed to have followed an acceptable, methodical sound way of coming up with their results or as said scientific method. This is what we call science today. They, in turn, may have referred to other people who had followed the same sound approach on things for their own books before them.

The important fact to note here is that we are compelled to build on what others have learned and corrected or adjusted it to fit new situations we come across. This is important as we do not have the time to learn everything from scratch in one lifetime. However, who do we believe in this? The people who said that this would occur if this was done in the past or someone just saying this is so without any justification to that end and not based on an acceptable approach in their conclusions as the validity of it is only available in the next life.

What we accept as correct in the scientific world is based on their qualifications or by knowing what they said in the past has now proven to be correct, and so the other things they have said should be true now. These qualifications we now call BS or BSC or Bachelor's degree, Master's degree or MSC, and of course the Ph.D. (Doctorate). We all expect the Ph.D. holders to go further than the knowledge they have acquired from their degree by engaging in more research in a specific area of their study and finding new things or postulate on something new which may have a strong chance of being justified by an acceptable approach to the subject in light of data they have collected.

During studies for a Bachelor's degree, we totally depend on what others had said as our lecturers would repeat what has been taught to students prior to us by learning from their teachers when they were students. They also recommend books which they themselves had studied from. During a master's degree program, which is a narrow area of study on a subject selected for the Bachelor's, we engage in research work of our own called a 'Thesis' as well as do a further deeper study on that selected subject guided by a relevant professor. For the Ph.D., it would mostly be further research on what has already been done for the Master's degree study to find something new or, at the least, postulate or present a new justifiable hypothesis.

This means, what one person has come up with in this hypothesis may be proven or refuted with time by others. As an example, a person may do his or her Bachelor's in the biology of living things, which include plants and animals with few other pertinent subjects. For their Master's, that person may do a deeper study of a narrower area, such as plant biology. For the Ph.D. research, they may undertake how specific plants absorb nutrients from their surroundings and postulate from experimental data that certain chemicals are needed in the water for the plant to absorb the water.

As mentioned before, a Master's degree is an acquired knowledge of both prior information on the subject selected and some research done on the same subject by oneself. They may also build on prior research done in this field but not necessarily finding something new. The Bachelor's degree is totally based on learning what others have stated, and the society has accepted as correct and subsequently taught in universities. The important factor to note here is the chain of events that occur where one learns from what others have said before and uses this data to build further on the same subject, which may be found to be incorrect later by another.

Meaning, we find that everything may only be absolutely true within a certain physical boundary of conditions and deemed incorrect out of this boundary of conditions. A classic example of the above said boundary of conditions is the Einstein theory of relativity, where the fastest thing in the universe is light. There was a time when it was considered as the gospel truth, but now as we go deeper into our understanding of the universe, it is no longer the gospel truth for all circumstances but only within a given framework of the happenings in the universe. Now, it has been found, as per quantum mechanics or science of subatomic particles, which we talked about earlier, that a photon, when entangled or inextricably linked with another photon, would change its status and replicate moves instantly irrespective of how far apart they are when its partner's status is changed. This means there is something much faster than light in this universe that we may not know of but is a fact.

Another example would be our understanding long ago that the electron, proton, and neutron are the smallest particles in the universe from which the atom was made. Deeper research done with the availability of more sophisticated apparatus, such as the cyclotron colliders, determined that they are made up of other particles, which are called Gluons, Quarks, etc. This, in turn, tells us that by building on the research of past Ph.D. graduates, our understanding of the world around science could get further refined with more sophisticated test equipment being made available to do further research.

For our physical requirements or to be useful for our economic wellbeing, the knowledge that the atom was made from electrons, protons, and neutrons was of much importance. This knowledge helped us with new inventions by understanding their functions through further research of the Ph.D.'s. This enabled us to synthesize new materials, such as different types of steel, plastic, and medicine, for the use of humanity for good or bad, but all these enhanced the economic activities and created more employment opportunities for the masses to make a living.

It is also noteworthy that science is not absolute all the time, as said before, but only correct within a said boundary of conditions. The Ph.D.'s would add more refinement to this with time by conducting more research. However, this may either enhance or restrict such boundary conditions. This reveals that even if we have faith in our Ph.D.'s, there is much more we do not know about what is happening in this universe. Additionally, we do all this through our minds. Our minds filter and purify our knowledge via more research that we learn with time.

Has anyone really thought of how we understand with our minds? It has been said that we teach our minds by observation from birth, correlating objects and actions with words, vision with pictures, etc. This information gets stored somewhere in the brain among the billions of nerve cell connections as sustained electrical energy. The other question now is, what initiated this action to happen? More importantly, how do we access this information when we require it? For example, when we are using a sharp knife, we automatically link this with danger. The danger of cutting yourself if used incorrectly, as experienced before or as been told by someone else. Again, is this an ability we carry from our birth?

Nevertheless, we do not know how this happens. For example, one does not say, "I see this now," and store it in a location in the brain. We do not even know how we command our brain to do what it must do when we need to run, walk, eat, etc. To this end, is there something outside of our body that detects the need and commands our brain to act accordingly?

In conclusion, the capabilities or traits in our mind determine the ability to earn our degrees, such as Bachelor's, Master's, or Ph.D. or none. This will, in turn, define how we contribute to our economy, as discussed earlier.

Chapter 9: Economy

Earlier, we mentioned the economy from time to time. The economy is also something we hear daily coupled with words such as recession, unemployment, banking crisis, stock market collapse, etc. In addition, volumes of books have been written on this subject, professors repeatedly talk of microeconomics to macroeconomics, but maybe this is something that does not make sense to some of us. Not to mention that our ability to survive also depends on how well our own economy is doing. To understand all this and the factors involved, we should take this from a simple scenario to a more complex situation.

Let us imagine that in this world, there are only two human beings: a good-looking man and a pretty woman. We will call them family as they would be sharing what they have and would be pleased with each other with all their needs met. For example, a perfect scenario would be the availability of plenty of freely accessible food, good health, shelter, and great weather too. They are content and have no further desires for anything else. In this situation, their economy can be considered 100% or near-perfect as they have all that they need and nothing else is desired but just to enjoy life as it is.

Let us assume that there are three humans now—a family of two and another individual who lacks food. Now food is not freely available, but everyone is expected to grow his or her own share of food. If we assume that the new person does not grow food, the economy is less than 100% as the person who does not grow food has no food to eat and is unable to buy food from the other two people and thus must live on the other person's charity. Further to the need for growing food, they need shelter now as the weather has changed, and sometimes it rains. Now, the person who does not grow food starts making things to meet all their shelter needs. Then this person gives what he makes to the food growers and gets food for himself. In this situation, we must assume that the food growers are always repairing their shelters as it continuously breaks, creating a **Demand** for the products made by the person who makes the shelter material. Also, this person has enough material around him or her to meet the demand for the said shelter material, which is called **Supply**. Hence, a key term in economics is **'Supply and Demand.'**

Furthermore, as they live close to each other, cultivate close by, and have material to build houses close by, they walk to each other's houses in a few minutes and **Trade** what each other have, and grow food to fulfill their needs. The term used for this type of trade is described as **Bartering**. Now, if the food growers and the housemaker do their share, do not get sick, have no need for clothes, or have no other desires, we would have a 100% economy again.

Now, we will assume there is another person in this group who is good at making clothing. Assuming the weather starts changing from the earlier perfect weather to rain or heat, they would need appropriate clothing, and the new person gets an opportunity to make clothes for all of them.

As before, the farming family grows food and barters it for housing material and clothing, and they now grow food sufficient to barter for clothes from the clothmaker as well as for the housing material. Now, as the farmer family would grow food for all, whilst the housemaker makes stuff for housing for all, and the clothmaker makes clothes for all. Now they all repair their houses as the house materials decay all the time, need clothes all the time as clothes wear out. This means there is still a demand for all their products all the time for all of them.

So, if all of them do what they are supposed to do and have the material they need to produce, live near to each other and have no other desires, the economy can be considered 100% again. **The supply meets the demand, and there is a demand for the supply all the time**.

Let us assume that there are ten people now, and some of them get sick sometimes. Also, this group now consists of four farmers, one medicine man, one clothmaker, one housemaker, one farm toolmaker, a jewelry-maker, and one bum who does nothing. Now, we assume that the demand for basic needs, such as food, has increased to more than the environment can supply, within easy reach of the farmers.

Someone in the group has gotten sick other than a farmer. A fear factor has come to the equation for all of them now. They all start fearing that the farmers would not be able to supply the food required by all if the farmers get sick as the farmers would not be able to farm or harvest the crops. Now, they will compete to give more of their products to the farmers to barter for the farmers' products for the purpose of **Hoarding** or some to be stored for future in the event there is a lack of food as food is essential to survive than any other need, such as roofing material or clothing, etc.

Farmers also may think that they, too, need to keep more food for themselves for the same reason and may not even want to sell what they currently harvest or have. This is not because the farmers got sick and could not provide the food required but the fear factor leading to **Speculations** of the possibility of an unexpected thing happening. When the possibility of sickness disappears, the fear factor also disappears. Importantly, this has brought to light the susceptibility of the economy to any unexpected situation and, in economic terms, what is called **Market Volatility**.

Assume that new development has taken place among these people with a newfound ego that requires the display of superiority over the others. The jeweler makes exquisite items using rare materials only some can afford despite everyone's desire in the community to possess them in the form of gold. Though economically, they do not bring any practical value to the sustenance of the community as food, clothes, or shelter would. Wearing jewels only enhances the ego of the people who possess them. This would be an indication to others of their superiority, like a king with his crown encrusted in jewels that others may not have. As most people in the group now want jewelry, they may use this as a hedge against bad times when they can barter the same to others in the community due to its imperishable nature.

Due to the families in this community having children, the number of members has now increased to a hundred, with an additional demand for essential items, such as food, clothing, and shelter. Now, there are more farmers, more clothmakers, more medicine men, and more jewelry-makers alongside a few who do not do anything and live on the generosity of others as the said bum.

Few things may happen now. There might be a reduction in the number of farmers someday as this is a difficult occupation requiring hard work in the sun and mud, and they may give up this trade due to this. On the other hand, the farmers may wish to produce more food as they see the demand for it has increased with more consumers. Due to difficulties in farming, the farmer might decide to produce the same amount of food and demand more for the products from others or try to produce more food and sell his products at the old barter rate as a generous and charitable human being and not human vulture or black marketeer.

The latter situation would be rare. The possibility would be that greed would take over the farmers' thinking. They would see an opportunity to ask for more items from the others for the same amount of food they wish to sell, especially nonperishable items, such as jewelry to enhance their self-ego, clothing, and even home construction products to make bigger, better houses for them. By this, some of the people in the community may even go hungry, being unable to produce enough to barter for the food required.

Now, we assume that in this situation, the farmers are kind and generous by deciding to produce more food and need additional tools to cultivate a larger area, which requires more of their food to barter for the tools. Their expenses have now increased, needing to produce higher amounts of food to meet the demand of all the people in the community. Now, we expect the economy to be 100% since everyone produces sufficient for the community and all the 100 people need their services or goods, which are sufficient for them all, with the bums too getting generous handouts from the producers of food, etc. Furthermore, there is the willingness of the people to look after the ones who are unable to work due to sickness and old age.

There may be a twist to this if we assume people do not get sick frequently. The medicine man cannot survive, as fewer people visit him for treatment and the economy goes down from 100%

again. The wise medicine man thinks that he will ask for more from the jewelry-maker since he cannot go anywhere to get medicine when he is sick, which is called a **Monopoly**. By doing this, he can keep the jewelry for a long time as they are imperishable and would have a continuous demand due to the ego of others in the community. Hence, he could barter this jewelry for his immediate or later needs. Now, the jeweler gets sick and goes to the medicine man, and the medicine man asks for more jewelry for his services, wherein the jeweler does not have and cannot produce much since he is sick. In this scenario, the production would not be sufficient to meet the current demand, which is termed as the **Imbalance in Supply and Demand**.

Had the jeweler produced and stored sufficiently when he could, this shortage of supply would not have occurred to meet the demand. On the other hand, the jeweler was sick and unable to produce more. Now, the jeweler decides to demand more of others' producers for his jewelry when he can make them. He would store them even temporarily and re-barter these items for what he needs when he gets sick. This leads to other people, such as the clothmaker, in turn, finding out that he must ask for more from the farmer or housemaker when they require his products. What we see here is a 100% perfect economy in harmony going into an imbalance of supply and demand, leading to what is known as **Inflation,** resulting in the increase of cost of resources required for their needs.

Now, we get into the situation of thousands of people in this group. As the population grows, they are now dispersed in a wider area for their housing, as they need more room to live by distancing themselves from one another. Let us assume that now not all the land of the area is suitable for human habitation or cultivation. With more land being required for cultivation, the farmers are compelled to go further away for cultivation. The housemaker would find that he must travel far to find material for his craft. As this happens, the citizens would find out that they would need a way or roads for transporting their goods, raw materials, and so on from where they are available to the location of making the final product. Alternatively, even if the product can be made where the raw material is available, the finished product now must be taken a long distance where the people are bartering. To this end, they would now need some sort of a device to move these items from the location where they are manufactured to where they are now needed.

An important thing to notice is that when people move to far locations to build their habitat, they are unable to travel long distances to obtain tools for their trade or resources for their occupation. Hence, they would have to carry large amounts of their products to other locations to barter as stated earlier, not knowing whether other people would require their products at this time, as there were no telephones or mobile phones during this time to know beforehand whether they need these products at this time.

This being the case, in the event the buyer does not want the product at that time, they would have to carry back the products or produce back to the point of manufacturing. Taking the case of the housebuilder, he would have to carry very heavy items to a distant location to the farmer to get his food, which may even take days. If the farmer does not require his products at this time, he would have to try another person (**Consumer**) who would require his product and possibly continue his travel, carrying his heavy products from place to place till he finds a **Buyer.**

Overall, he would not have much time to make his own products to barter because of having to carry a load of produce from one point to the other, wasting time. This forced people to bring their produce to a centralized location where they could barter their products more efficiently. Thus, the concept of a **Market** was born. All the people in one area now came to this single location to barter their products for their separate needs. Sometimes even to store any excess produce in a nearby location where they could easily take them back to the market again when required. These locations were known as **Warehouses.**

Now another issue has cropped up. Someone must protect the produce brought to the warehouse by the farmer, housemaker, etc. This situation is more critical, for example, during a drought as there would be a shortage of resources, especially food, and the need arises for people to protect what they already have from people within, like the bum or even other such groups of people.

This situation forces these people to organize themselves into groups to protect themselves. Furthermore, there would be the need to resolve disputes over the resources among themselves, and hence, the requirement for a system to keep **Law and Order** in the community arose. To this end, the communities would define the do's and don'ts, which become law, and agree on punishments for those who do not follow or break them.

This then requires these groups to appoint people designated as Judges, Policemen, Military, or Prison Guards to manage the prisoners when the Judges send them for punishment when the laws are broken. To oversee all this, a leader, such as a **King** or **Queen** in ancient times or **President** or **Prime Minister** in modern times, is elected to coordinate and assume this leadership role. However, the king or the appointee cannot do everything by themselves and thus appoints a group of people called the advisers or cabinet to look after each aspect of the community. In modern days, this group of people is what we call **Government,** which only administers and consumes but does not produce anything for the economy.

However, there is an issue now for this non-producing organization we earlier named government – how to provide essential items, such as food, to the people working for the government, such as police, military, judges, and jailors, for them to meet their basic needs for survival. This, of course, had to come from the people of the community or society who are under the control or jurisdiction of this government. Such resources collected by the government from the people under its authority, for the people working for the government is called **Tax** or **Taxation**.

The government then sends agents to collect taxes from the people, which may be made up of a certain amount of food from the farmer, part of the clothing from the clothmaker, etc., at certain intervals of time. They even collected part of whatever the people bring to the market to sell. The markets were generally located in the king's palace or where the government offices were located.

Something to remember now is, once the people form this government and the government become the people, all the land would automatically come under the authority of the government, irrespective of some of it being owned by others in the community. Therefore, the government has the right to confiscate anything belonging to anyone at will, including land, even if a farmer claims ownership of his land as his own if it comes within the overall umbrella of ownership of the government. If one did not pay taxes, the government would send its agents to confiscate something that the person owns, even their property in the form of land, a house, or whatever they can lay their hands on or even send them to prison.

Now, there is an issue with what the government collects as taxes. Some of these items may be perishable as meat, fish, vegetables, etc., that must be immediately dispersed to the government workers as they cannot be stored for a long time. On the other hand, some of these items would be too bulky to handle, such as the roof-maker's products like tiles or rafters. These items given to the people working for the government are what we call **Wages** or **Salaries.** Another important issue the government faced was to quantify the wages being paid to the employees. How can you quantify a basket of grain against a rafter for a roof? Since items collected were difficult to quantify and handle, it led to the need for another mode of paying these wages. Hence, the concept of **Money** came into existence.

For centuries, people have been fascinated with gold. This may be due to its rarity and non-perishability to having a permanent luster, though it had no personal benefit to humans other than for adornment or some industrial applications. It is neither consumable nor known as a medicine and cannot be worn as clothes or used as a shelter because it is rare and only found in small quantities. However, people were ready to kill and even invade nations for this metal just because of its rarity, glowing color, non-fading glitter, non-perishability, and ease of molding. As such, they made it into objects to be worn or stored in safe places when found. However, this did not only apply to gold but silver also due to its similar properties. However, silver was more naturally available than gold and hence, did not have a demand like gold. Copper, too, was used similarly but was more in abundance and would tarnish or lose its luster with time in a process called oxidation and became less valuable.

Now, the government at that time, controlled by the appointed head called king or queen, confiscated most of these metals from their subjects and subsequently gave them to its employees to be used for purchasing their needs from the farmer or the clothmaker or others, as said before. To replenish the stock of gold and silver, the appointed head demanded taxes to be paid to the government in this gold, silver, or copper from the merchants in return.

Now, valued by all his subjects and being a malleable metal, the king quantified the metal and called it **Coins**. The king could now easily pay his soldiers, judges, and police officers in near-exact amounts every time he needed to pay their wages. In return, his subjects used the same to purchase their needs from the market by paying with these coins; for example, one gold coin would be worth a bag of corn. Most importantly, all the people in the kingdom now tried to hoard these gold, silver, or copper coins, knowing they could use them whenever they wish to purchase anything they wanted. Also, they knew that the supply of these metals of the coins was limited. More importantly, everybody knew the only way anyone could earn these coins was by producing what another person wanted. In other words, 'having to work for it.' This made the coins more valuable. This value of the coins was termed as the **Purchasing Power** of the money.

Now, the population grew up to millions with more children born, and all of them in the time needed to produce something or provide a service that others wanted to earn this money. We now know the basic means as to how people make their money now as being farmers, doctors, engineers, laborers, and government employees or business people like traders, etc. Apart from this, there were people who manufactured tools for the farmers and made vehicles or carts for transportation (for goods and people) and the like. This created more opportunities and needs for other products, such as parts for the cart manufacturers, iron for wheels, and leather for harnesses for the carts, etc.

In the world of economy, these activities can be categorized under a few headings, such as farming, manufacturing, services, and the bureaucracy or the government. Farmers, we know. Manufacturers are the people who utilize the abundance of nature to form objects for the benefit of people; for example, the usage of steel to make plows, enabling the farmers to till more land and earn more money in order to produce more food with less labor and time. Or else use steel to build carts so that the farmer could easily transport his goods to the market in larger quantities. Services were provided by the doctors, engineers, bricklayers, carpenters, hospital services staff, firefighters, bus drivers, train drivers, cleaners, etc. Bureaucracy and government are what we have already discussed before.

The service industry, for example, supports the maintenance of roads, makes buildings for people, offers drivers to drive transport vehicles, and so on with the doctors, nurses looking after the health of the people, etc. The bureaucracy includes all the people working for the government, such as the police, judiciary, senators, House of Representatives, and all the ministries, including the president or prime minister. They help maintain law and order and supposedly guide the economic development for everyone towards their betterment (an interesting concept that we will investigate later under government). This is by enacting and enforcing laws for the benefit of the masses using the police, military, and judiciary when and if required to enforce them. Hence, such laws supposedly allow the farmers, manufactures, builders, businessmen, etc. to conduct their businesses safely without fear of being robbed, or in other words, it gives them the opportunity to make money without fear if they keep on paying taxes to the government to keep this bureaucracy alive.

Now that order has been established for people to go about with their businesses safely by the government, there is an important issue here. Not everyone can be a farmer, doctor, or engineer. If this happens, there would be no clothes, medicine, or would have a shortage of it. There must be a **Balance**, for example, how many farmers or doctors are needed in a society. There should not be too many of them or only a few of them. Another example is, if one farmer produces all the food for the millions in that society, then it would wipe out the opportunity for many more to earn a living by farming. Reflecting on this situation, we use the term **Economy** more seriously here than earlier. Meaning, the study of a multitude of factors taken together is what affects the earning capacity of all the people in a society.

As said earlier, what happens if a few farmers produce all the food requirements, few cloth manufacturers make clothes for everyone, a few housebuilders make building products for all, and if few doctors look after all the people? How do the other people in the community get to earn money? They need to invent something or work for someone who manufactures things or provides a service to the society like doctors or hospitals do, or they can even be someone providing leisure activities, such as cinemas, restaurants, etc. Some can also make things to satisfy the ego of the said rich, such as yachts, jewelry, etc. In time, however, opportunities to work in these industries get saturated, possibly leaving many people in the community unemployed.

This need gives rise to **Inventions** or ideas for new products and **Discoveries,** or even the need of finding new enhancements to things already existing, which one can make use of better than before. For example, we could see the evolution of the motor car, whose manufacturing provides various employment opportunities to people. The entrepreneurs use these inventions or discoveries and manufacture products for use by the masses, giving rise to what is known as **Industries**. Invariably, they would become what we call rich. Meaning, they will have more than enough money for all their physical as well as ego requirements, such as buying private planes for travel, luxury cars, luxury homes, or even leave vast wealth for their children, etc.

The rich also employ other people in their factories and pay them wages or salaries for their services. This they use to buy food and other needed products from others to sustain them and their families and maybe for some limited personal enjoyment also. This cycle of events of manufacturing gave rise to what we call the **Industrial Revolution**, the true birth of the term 'Economy.' In the past, there have been different phases of this distinct industrial revolution due to various discoveries or inventions, such as the wheel, steel, electricity, steam engines, and combustible engines, etc. making way for automobiles, aircraft, ships, computers, the internet, and mobile phones and many other as used today.

Industrial revolution

With the birth of industrialization and the increase in the world population, it was difficult to have gold and silver as the tender for purchases due to its scarcity. Some countries started using copper as a lesser denomination tender due to its respective abundance than gold and silver. Also, copper does not corrode like iron and has always been a scarce source only to an extent. With the expansion of population and subsequent organization of people to countries defined by boundaries, a new form of currency for bartering or purchasing was essential as silver and gold were not abundant or even available in all countries. Higher denominations were also needed as people started trading in large volumes of goods.

Thus, the concept of **Paper Money** originated, where everyone in a country represented by a king, president, or prime minister authorized the use of paper money as the official currency for purchases. However, in this case, anyone could have printed money, making it worthless. Thus, the authorities employed secret technology using special paper and printing techniques to prevent everyone from printing money. This, of course, did not still prevent some people from attempting to print paper money in various ways. To deter this, legal measures were put in place to severely punish offenders trying to duplicate the valid currency authorized and printed by the government.

Now, the question is, why cannot the governments keep printing more money as they wish? If this happens, the people would be flushed with money and be willing to pay more and more money for limited resources, competing to buy those resources for survival or even for entertainment. In this situation, the purchasing power of money would decrease quickly. As an example, let us take the situation of a bread-maker or baker.

Assume that the baker wanted ten units of paper money or what we now call **Cash** for a loaf of his bread. Now due to the sudden scarcity of flour, he is only able to make less bread. However, people still need the same amount of bread for consumption. As the bread is now an essential item for survival, the baker would increase the value of the bread in order to earn more money, or maybe because he must pay more for the flour. Now the people who could afford it may even bid for the same bread. Say offer fifteen units of paper money for the same loaf of bread. Therefore, as the scarcity of basic resources increases, there will be a reduction in the purchasing power of paper money, putting the phenomenon called inflation in effect.

Nevertheless, if there is less demand for essential resources as per our example, perhaps due to a surplus of flour the baker has bought, he now needs to utilize this excess flour within a period before it goes bad. Hence, he would make more bread, but the demand may be the same at the current price he sold the bread before. To overcome this situation, the baker will reduce the price of his bread, encouraging those who previously did not want the bread to buy it. This means the same amount of paper money could now buy more resources, and this phenomenon is termed **deflation**.

The aspect of inflation, which we will discuss later, is such that in some countries like Italy or Japan, to purchase some items, you need to pay a million units of their currency. So, imagine the situation if the money comes only in denominations of 1, 10, and 100 notes, and you must pay 100,000 units of money for a loaf of bread. The people would have to carry this paper money in large bundles, which is not practical in day-to-day life for the masses. Hence, to avoid this burden to the masses, many zeros are now included in the lowest denomination of paper money. For example, the earliest paper currency unit was one unit; now, it is1000 units. In some instances, entire paper money is replaced with new paper money, which is valued at a higher rate by the government of that nation to avoid this situation.

As mentioned earlier, people who did not farm or produce essential items had to find a way to make money. In other words, some of them had to live by working for institutions as police officers, soldiers, judges, or university lecturers, which was affiliated with the government or its civil service unit. This gave birth to what we call **Bureaucracy,** as mentioned before, meaning that they would not be easily fired or laid off and the authority for monitoring their performance was also a government unit. Sometimes, another such bureaucracy manages them. This is unless the public clamors for change, stating the need to oversee the spending to maintain them or what they spend on, especially when the economy turns bad. Or when the government finds it difficult to pay them due to less collection of taxes from the working people. All in all, it is the public perception in general that some of such institutions are a waste of taxpayers' money.

On the other hand, there is a reason for bureaucracy as the people working for the government have to adhere to strict procedures to ensure there is no pilferage or abuse of authority. This is due to them being under a less responsible overseeing authority than a privately owned organization. As said before, government employees do not lose their jobs easily for low performance because they monitor themselves. Furthermore, their topmost overseeing authority changes when the government changes, and hence, these higher authorities would not care less as it is all taxpayers' money and not theirs.

However, in a private organization, the owner or owners of the business try to ensure maximum output from their employees in order to make the highest profit possible. To the minimum, at least ensure that their investment is not lost, ending up in **Bankruptcy**. The existence of these private institutions is to make as much wealth or money as possible for their owners and to survive in a competitive economy. Hence, they can be **Optimally Geared** to this end. Whilst bureaucratic institutions tend to be money-losing institutions or not performing to their optimal capacity. However, it is to be noted that the government bureaucracy does not exist to make money or profit, but at least it is expected to function efficiently and effectively to meet its objectives at a reasonable cost to the masses.

As mentioned before, people who did not farm, work for the government, or make essential items, tend to make things that were not important for the masses to survive but to satisfy their ego, for pleasure, or convenience, in anticipation of having a market for these products. These would be like making fancy food, drinks, perfume, paintings, cosmetics, films, or music, etc. It was up to their imagination to make it if it could be sold. This was at their free will and not forced by anyone. It was also made at their own risk, not knowing if they were able to sell or even make a profit. Such risk-taking is an important pathway for people to find an avenue of income generation.

Taking a risk to either gain a profit or, in the worst case, to bear a loss is the fundamental basis of **Capitalism.** This has been an inadvertent practice of people for a long time. They would make something and bring it to the market to sell in the hope that people would buy. This could have been a simple thing as a food item. If they did not sell, they had to take it back and suffer the consequence of the loss of their investment in making whatever they brought to the market. On the other hand, if it got sold, another person too would now make the same thing to sell in the market. Now, they had to compete by either making better products than the other person or lower the price. This is also a fundamental principle in the capitalist system called **Competition.**

Under a capitalist economy, people are empowered to attempt different ways to make money for themselves even if there is no initial demand. However, they anticipate a hike in demand once the product is made or the service is made available. However, the person who makes such items is expected to assess the market for the new product through **Market Research**. In other words, a person who wants to make a new food item, such as a bun, may make fewer items to assess the demand for it before making more. In the same token, if the first item does not sell, this person may change the product slightly and try again, perhaps by adding a little sugar to the top of the bun. These people are called **Entrepreneurs,** the backbone of capitalism, fulfilling a critical function in the system to sustain the economy, which we will discuss later.

Earlier, we talked about a person selling the buns they made in the market. The word 'selling' here means trying to convince a person to buy that bun through person-to-person contact. This is like someone coming to a house, selling cookies. However, now this person wants to increase his sales of the bun as he or she realizes that there is a market or demand for the bun. Hence, his intention now will be to reach a larger audience to sell these buns on a large scale.

In this case, he must get a message out to the masses that he is selling buns and, if interested, how and where people can buy them. This is called **Marketing**. For this, the primary tool used is called **Advertising**. We see this every day on TV, billboards, and the internet. Through advertising, people try to convince a potential buyer how good their product is for its purpose and that it is available at a valued price. Now here, the term 'valued' is important. This means that the targeted user should think that they are paying a fair price for this. For example, if the seller is selling the buns to the average person, he cannot price it above the price of other buns in the market unless it is bigger, tastier, etc. or there is a feature in this bun that stands above the rest, and yet the bun is still affordable by the targeted users.

However, even if these entrepreneurs have an idea to make something they could sell, they may lack money to purchase the raw material, equipment, hire people, or acquire land to locate their businesses for this large-scale endeavor. This may lead them to borrow money from other people by convincing them that this new product will be successful as per the market research.

People who lend money request more money at the time of repayment, as there is a risk involved in lending if the new endeavor fails. The extra money the lender requests is known as **Interest.** To ensure the lender gets his money back, he may take temporary ownership of any non-moveable assets of the borrower, such as land, house, or even gold, if the borrower has any. In the event the borrower does not pay back with interest, the borrower also authorizes the lender to sell any of these assets to recover with interest the money borrowed. The amount of money lent is called the **Principal**. This situation even applies to what we call corporations.

We will discuss later how corporations came into being. As for now, suffice to say, corporations are groups of people working as single units of entrepreneurs. They run large-scale manufacturing businesses in the factories they may own. Sometimes they are service providers, such as airlines. These corporations, too, will have the need to borrow money, and one single individual may not have such large amounts to lend. In a situation such as this, in order to meet this demand, groups of people with money came together to make dedicated institutions called **Investment Banks.** Investment banks only lent to corporations.

At the lower scale, they are called just **Banks**, which also perform the same function but deal with ordinary borrowers or small-scale entrepreneurs. In both situations, their business is to lend money and make money on the money lent, which we called interest. The interest earned is shared among the shareholders of the bank or with the depositors—a minimum amount or even nothing but the safety of their money.

As said, banks opened their businesses to ordinary people to deposit their money for safekeeping, which is their primary function. For this, they sometimes give a small interest but mainly guarantee the safety of depositors' money and offer them the convenience of using debit cards for cashless purchases to this end. As such, the depositors feel safe as the bank takes the responsibility to provide 24/7 protection for the money, which normal people cannot do by themselves due to its cost. The ordinary people who deposit their money in these banks are the **Depositors.** The justification of little for the depositor and more for the bank shareholder comes with the concept of risk. This means, in general terms, if the borrower's business goes down, it is the bank's money that is lost and not the depositor's.

However, the banks also take temporary possession of collateral from the borrower, such as his land, house, etc., unless they consider the business that is borrowing the money to be of exceptionally low risk. This is to ensure that, in the event of the borrower defaulting on the loan, they would be able to sell these assets to recover the money as well as provide the depositors confidence of getting their money back eventually.

Normally, the value of the asset held as collateral is to be much higher than the loan given. This ensures that the lender could dispose of the asset easily with minimum risk in the event the borrower defaults on the loan payback. Hence, banks ensure their survival in adversity and are said to be an engine of the growth of the economy. At the same time, banks ensure the stability of the economy, as well as safeguard depositors' money.

With time, competition among the banks increased to lend to the most profitable and secure businesses. This sometimes led some banks to lend large sums of money without collateral, considering them to be of low risk due to the large profits they make. It is important to note that banks must lend to make a profit as interest on their lending to cover their own expenses for utilities, salaries of staff, building cost, etc., at the minimum, before gaining a profit for its shareholders in the main.

If the bank does not lend and only has expenses, then the shareholders (we will discuss this term later) and depositors could become agitated. This is because they would lose what they have invested in the bank and may even want to withdraw their money out of the bank. This may cause a bad financial situation for the bank, which is known as **Insolvent** or, in simple terms, 'owes more than what it has in hand as cash or what it can immediately convert to cash.' This means, whatever that entity has as capital or assets, such as the buildings it owns, is not sufficient to cover its immediate financial obligations, such as rent, wages of employees, taxes, etc.

Sometimes, it is important to note that this situation does not necessarily mean the banks do not have money as assets. Banks mostly lend on a long-term basis. Once the bank lends the depositors money to borrowers, that money is tied up. The bank earns interest on the money lent, with some of the principal given back to the bank in installments. This is because the entrepreneur or the businessperson may buy machinery, land, etc., for expansion of his business or for a new business venture. This may or may not make money or a profit immediately but only helps to make the product he wants, which would hopefully provide them with a profit in time.

However, the terms entrepreneur and businessperson are essentially not the same. The entrepreneur tends to develop new products or innovate, whereas the term businessperson may even apply to someone who just buys a product and sells the same at a higher price. For example, a businessperson may buy some old furniture in one location of the country and polish or clean it and sell the same product at another location at a higher price. In this book, we mostly refer to entrepreneurs who fuel the engine of growth or the economy much more than businesspersons do.

Then there is another lending institution called **Finance Companies** that lend money at a much higher interest rate than the banks. They take higher risks than banks in the money lending process. They also give a higher interest than banks to the depositors. These companies do not hold any fixed assets of the borrower. However, sometimes the finance company will hold what we call a 'note' from the borrower or ownership of the item that the borrower purchased until that person pays off the loan with interest.

This is mostly applicable to vehicles. Finance companies may cease these vehicles if the borrower defaults. This is because they solely depend on the borrower's credit history rather than the borrower's business or entrepreneurship skills to lend the funds. Therefore, the risk is higher because, even if the vehicle, for example, is seized or taken back by the finance company, the vehicle may be in bad condition, making it impossible to sell and recover all the money lent.

A situation like this may lead to the sudden closure of such companies with vast losses to the depositors who took a risk to get a higher interest rate than what was offered by the regular banks. This happens when the economy sometimes goes bad, and people lose their jobs, unable to pay for the loans on cars or other white goods, such as fridges, washing machines, and furniture, etc.

With less stringent regulations governing such finance companies, malpractices by the owners are higher compared to the banks. These companies mainly cater to the consumer market as said and indirectly contributed to the economy, but they may lead to their own failure when people lose their jobs and cannot pay them back for the goods purchased under finance. It contributes to the economy by helping the consumer to buy products immediately and create demand for such products an entrepreneur has made or businesspeople provide.

On the other hand, if this facility was not there, then the public would have to collect money for a period of time to purchase the same equipment, and in the meantime, the said equipment might become obsolete, and the new one may be more expensive. In other words, one may never get to enjoy the benefits of products, such as refrigerators, washing machines, and color TV. This ability to be able to buy a consumer product immediately is a particularly important aspect affecting the economy as it keeps the factories busy providing employment to the masses.

Let us look at an example. A new phone has come to the market, and this person does not have immediate cash to buy it. Therefore, he gets a loan from the finance company and buys it to make use of it immediately. He starts paying back the finance company with a higher interest rate than the bank, and in time, he pays off the finance company. By this time, a better phone has come to the market. Now this person discards the old phone and buys the new one or sells the old one for a lesser price than purchased.

The phone-maker has now sold two phones. Otherwise, he may have only sold one phone, or none, as the buyer must keep collecting money to buy one phone while at the same time new phones keep on entering the market at higher prices. In the end, this person would never be able to buy a phone as he may still be collecting money. Furthermore, another important feature of finance companies is that they provide small loans and not big loans like the banks. If the borrower defaults the payback, their names would be blacklisted according to a credit reporting method, and they would not be able to borrow any more money or get credit to buy more stuff.

Furthermore, these finance companies do not give money physically to the borrower and at the same time charge a percentage of the product selling price from the seller called commission. This is apart from the interest charged from the borrow to buy the product. This scenario increases the immediate **Purchasing Power** of the masses, though it seems this method seems ruthless for the poor, who are the customers of these finance companies in the main. We have now seen how these finance companies contribute to the economy of the country.

In a negative sense, the lenders can saturate the purchasing power of the buyer if they are not careful in their lending practice by lending to those who are not financially able to pay back the principal. Exorbitant interest is charged on any payment defaults. This is a financial trap that people sometimes find difficult to get out of.

During a **Recession**, which we will discuss later, some borrowers will be forced to default their payments to the finance company. This situation will ruin the borrower's credit history. When this happens, it will have a detrimental effect on the economy. Consider the situation where employed people who are buying lots of stuff on credit (finance) face unexpected unemployment due to mass layoffs because of an upcoming recession. Large masses of people will not be able to pay back their obligations to the finance companies. They are blacklisted, and even if the situation gets better, the purchasing power of these people would be lost for a long time even if they pay off their debt.

As history tells us, sometimes even sound businesses collapse, taking the banks down with them, causing loss of money for the ordinary depositors, which leads to the uprising of the masses to the loss of faith in the economy of the country, which if it happens, become a grave situation to the country concerned. To soothe things out to a certain extent, the government steps in with a limited guarantee to the small depositors of their money. This would give confidence to the ordinary people to deposit their money in the banks again. At the same time, the government will monitor the functioning of the banks as well as introduce laws to stop banks from making risky investments on ordinary depositor's money. If not for this oversight, a large shareholder of a bank could lend ordinary people's money to a failing business they own or to someone they know without collateral and subsequently declare bankruptcy, siphoning depositor's money for them or their accomplices.

A notable fact of this situation is that one must have something of value to borrow money from the bank unless you have a good record of past achievements available to get the bank's confidence. However, this could restrict an entrepreneur who has no assets for collateral but only good ideas or inventions for a product or service that the public would most positively purchase. To fill this void so they could have the necessary funds to bring their products to the market, the concept of the **Stock Market** was born.

This is where the entrepreneur offers **Shares** or a percentage of ownership of his or her business to the general public in return for cash or **Capital** to start the business where the percentage of shares dictates the **ROI (Return on Investment)** or the percentage of the profit of the new business. This, of course, depends on how well this entity would function, and hence the birth of a concept called **Company** was introduced. In this case, ROI is expected to be higher than what a bank offers, but of higher risk as the business may not succeed and even may lose all the wealth of the shareholders. Now, we have the concept of the **High-Risk High-Return Principle,** a pillar of a capitalist economy (types of economies we will discuss later).

With time, there was an opportunity for the public to own different types of shares of a company as **Ordinary Shares, Preference Shares, and Non-Voting Shares,** etc. However, we will not go into details of these different types of shares as the objective of this book is to provide the interconnectivity of economics and faith or beliefs, but not the details of the former. Similarly, there are different investment options on the stock market called **Derivate**, **Margins,** etc., that are not emphasized here due to the said focus of this book.

Now, in this situation, the investor becomes part-owner of the company, exposing themselves to damage claims by the end-users of the company's product if something bad happens to the end-user. An example would be a drug manufactured by a pharmaceutical company, causing severe side effects or even death to a patient even if used as per the prescription instructions. The patient will now sue the company owners for large damages, driving the company to bankruptcy and forcing the shareholders to pay money out of their own pocket as damages to the so affected.

This discouraged the public from investing or be a shareholder of such companies, starving them of funds for starting a new business and thus affecting the growth of the economy. To minimize this effect on the ordinary shareholder, the government made a law that limited the liability of the company to a predetermined value only and deterred the public from suing for damages against the private wealth of the shareholders. However, most of these companies, called LLC or limited liability companies, are still initiating entrepreneurship and dynamism to be a strength to the economy.

In a company, we have the concept of a CEO or Chief Executive Officer, Board of Directors, and the said shareholders. However, the shareholders do not normally have a say on the decisions made by the company for its day-to-day operations but may raise issues during the annual shareholders meeting or vote to get rid of the CEO or any other if not satisfied with their performance.

An important distinction here is that ordinary people are now asked to risk their savings on companies or businesses that do not have much information on how the company is being run and would blame the government if these companies go bust. This will negatively affect large masses of people if allowed to happen, not to mention such an effect on the ability of entrepreneurs to raise money to take our economy forward, who are also the pillars of our economy.

Thus, the concept of **Rating Companies,** such as Standard & Poor's, PricewaterhouseCoopers, etc., was established to counter this situation. Their job was to investigate the financial health of such companies and rate them so that the public would have a basis to measure the risk in investing their hard-earned money in these companies.

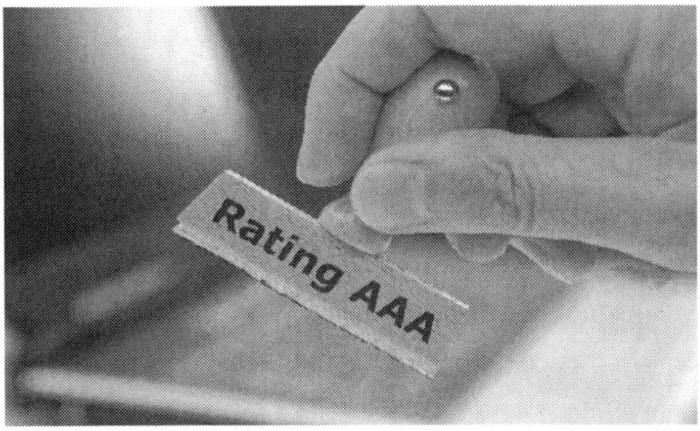

These rating companies could identify companies with a higher probability of ROI and ensure the least risk to the shareholders by investigating their financial performance on a short and long-term basis. They would rate the companies 'A's to 'C's etc., where 'A' would be of less risk to C' being higher risk. These ratings encouraged businesses to have a sound financial footing and to ensure they have funds available from investors for expansion of their businesses or even day-to-day operations rather than borrowing money from the banks at a higher interest rate.

The better a company does financially, the more profit it makes, and if it also has a good long-term certification from a rating company for sound financial growth forecast, more people will want to buy shares of that company. Demand for and price of shares of such companies increase. Similarly, if the opposite happens, the price of the shares goes down with less demand. When required, shareholders can sell their shares for a higher amount than their purchase price if these companies do better later, as stated above.

One may even consider this as a gamble. Even with positive ratings a company may have, it can unexpectedly go bankrupt. For example, a company selling umbrellas in a very rainy country may pay high dividends or interest on its shares. Suddenly, a drought comes, and umbrella sales go down. With reduced sales and still having to pay the employees, building rent, etc. which is now called **Overhead,** they may not have an option but to declare bankruptcy, losing even the shareholders' money.

With the human desire to gamble, we find some people known as **Speculators** who try to make money from the stock market by manipulating it. They gamble on whether a particular company's stock or share price may go up or down, not taking into consideration the current performance but possible occurrence in the future. This can be done in several ways. Anyone can buy shares of any company from the stock market if a company is listed in the stock market by paying a commission to a dealer to this end. However, nowadays, some dealers offer such services even free of charge with some other ways of compensation to them.

Now going back to the issue of gambling with the stock market, for example, some people may assume that the demand for oil is going to increase due to an impending war in an oil-producing country. With war, there would be less oil coming to the market from this country, causing a hike in the price of this oil. They would then buy shares or stocks of other fuel-producing companies in the hope that when the fuel price goes up, the profit of these companies will increase, translating to higher returns on their shares.

However, this may not happen at all if the current oil-producing countries increase their oil output, meeting the current demand. This will stabilize the price in the market. However, if lucky, the company they bought the shares of may get more revenue by selling more oil instead of via higher prices, hence more profit for the shareholders. On the other hand, if they are unable to sell more oil due to other oil-producing countries taking this slack, this company's share price may fall as investors would switch to buy shares of those companies.

You could also sell the stock of a company immediately upon receiving bad news relating to that company, such as an anticipated increase in the price of raw material, which the company requires for making their products. As of now, this company's product price would have to go up. Hence, fewer people would buy this product, resulting in low profits for that company and fewer dividends for its shareholders. Some argue that this is a good situation for the economy as it prevents or reduces exposure of the company to such situations in the future and makes them more careful in their activities, which means not exposing one's business to a single supplier of raw materials or services. Thereby, they can bid for lower prices for their raw materials among different suppliers. Some say this is another positive thing in the capitalist or somewhat socialist system of the economy as the competition among sellers of end products or suppliers of any kind keeps the prices low and of better quality for the consumers.

People working at the company's highest level get firsthand knowledge of what is going to happen to the company before the public. This knowledge will be especially important to the shareholders. If something good is going to happen, they would immediately buy more shares and, when this good news becomes public, would sell the same at a higher price. Similarly, when something bad is going to happen, they will sell the shares immediately before they lose their value.

This knowledge of what is happening within the company is especially important to ordinary shareholders or even outside stock market gamblers. Hence these companies are legally bound to keep this information secret due to stiff penalties or even jail time for the culprits for premature disclosure to limited groups of people within or outside the company until the public is so informed.

Hence, for an outsider, it is valuable to receive this information as it would either make them avoid losses or earn a better profit. Therefore, having someone within the company with this information and using the same to buy or sell stocks before the public knows is called **Insider Trading,** a term we hear in the newspapers from time to time. To prevent such situations, the government has introduced penalties to those people found guilty of such activity and has introduced an institution called the **Exchange & Securities Commission** to monitor such happenings.

Now, a simple concept of providing an opportunity for entrepreneurs to find the money for their business has become more complicated because as it is affected by the activities of the aforesaid people who make it a gambling den.

Also, even a good company could be razed to the ground by baseless rumors if spread effectively. People would then sell their shares at lower prices, enabling whom I call **Vulture Capitalist** to buy up that company below the actual market value of that company. These people then sell off the valuable parts of that good company in pieces, including the machinery, building, etc., to make a large profit to the determinant of its former employees.

Some can argue that this is a good thing for the economy as it puts the owners of the companies on guard to make them perform well all the time. However, it is the opinion of the author that this is not the case as the harm caused by these actions outweigh any such perceived benefits. For example, it is a fact that all companies do undergo financial constraints some time or the other because of global or other reasons beyond their control. However, in time, most of these companies recover and go on to providing employment for many, contributing to the development of the economy of our society.

It is noteworthy that when a company is broken up and sold, it benefits only a handful of people and cuts off the distribution of wealth or money back to society, which is the driver of a good economy. An exception to this situation would be when the vulture capitalist sells off the nonperforming part of the company and retains the profitable part or the one that still has the potential to perform better. This is, of course, prevents the company from being dragged down into bankruptcy by the non-profitable part of that company or business. Here, the vulture capitalist sees an opportunity to put more money into this business to make it profitable or even make it lean and mean or reduce costs in some way (most of the time by reducing staff) and make the unprofitable part profitable again, saving the company as a whole and many of its employees' livelihood. These people now become Venture Capitalists and not Vulture Capitalists.

Bankruptcy is when a company can no longer have cash or can no longer borrow money from anywhere to meet its obligations to its creditors or employees, such as wages. Under this situation, the company can close its doors, declaring itself bankrupt and sell the assets it has, and pay off its creditors with whatever is left of the sale of its assets. This may not be the full amount due, but whatever is possible. Alternatively, if lucky, the company can be bought over by a competitor for a better price than whatever they could raise by selling off their assets.

Nevertheless, sometimes, due to sudden large-scale bankruptcies, the government comes up with different versions of bankruptcies called **Chapter 11**. This is due to the mass unemployment created when a multitude of company's go bankrupt at the same time, causing a shock in the economy. The objective here is to give the company in financial difficulty time to reorganize themselves or cut its operating costs to be profitable again with a possible settlement of its existing debt at a lesser rate of the dollar or postpone its immediate debt till a later date when it expects to be profitable again.

Now, we have seen that the stock market gives the opportunity for ordinary people to raise money to start a business. Most importantly, to borrow the money at zero interest but pay on earnings or on shares issued to the investors. This is in instances where the banks would not lend, or the company would not want to borrow money from a bank and get tied down to the fixed time of repayment of the interest or the capital or both. With regards to the shareholders, the company is not forced to meet such deadlines.

However, the shareholders would be expecting interest or dividends on their investment in due course more than a bank would give for their deposits.

As discussed earlier, the primary need for the stock market was to have a place entrepreneurs can approach to raise money for their new business by offering part ownership of the new company through what is called shares or stocks. This was due to the banks' lack of confidence in the business prospering, or the risk was really high even if they lent at a higher interest rate. Not to mention, they would not have the security of fixed assets from these entrepreneurs or even a personal guarantee from a person who the bank would consider having 'good standing' with the bank, meaning a person or entity currently having a good business relationship with the bank who can provide a fixed asset as **Collateral** against the bank loan to the entrepreneur, allowing the bank to sell this collateral to recover their loan in the event of default or nonpayment of the loan.

For fledgling entrepreneurs, initial capital is hard to find even going to the stock market as that person has nothing to show the investors as a product and may only have an idea. Now, for the entrepreneur who does not have the startup funds but has a good invention, there are some people ready to assist. They're called **Venture Capitalists,** who are willing to provide this funding on a note, meaning IOU, or through ownership of a part of the company, like a shareholder, based on the expectation of earning higher profits eventually after taking into consideration the capitalistic principle 'higher risk and higher return.' This, as mentioned before, is also a foundation pillar for capitalism.

Now, even if the entrepreneur has the funding from the venture capitalist, the bank, or the stock market to make the product or provide the service, there is a situation as to how to inform the people of this product for them to buy it if it is made on a large scale. Of course, if it is only a few units of a product, they could go door-to-door to sell them. However, with large-scale production, things are different. If one makes the best product for a certain application, but the masses do not know about this product, it will not sell much. On the other hand, if the product is not that good, but the masses know about it, one could expect some sales. This shows the high importance of making the product known to the masses or its expected end-users. As said before, this is done by marketing, which is an industry by itself.

This concept of marketing means mainly advertising via TV, the Internet, and Billboards to notify the potential buyers of the product being manufactured and capture their attention to the advertiser's message. Currently, marketing has become a large industry. It provides employment opportunities to vast amounts of people, such as artists to draw pictures for billboards, billboard-makers, market researchers, actors to say how good the product is on the TV, website designers to make webpages promoting the product, etc. All this contributes to the economy by direct employment as well as assisting the manufacturer in selling its product to consumers, thus, keeping the economy rolling.

Therefore, the bottom line is that a good economy is an opportunity for every member of the public who wants to earn a living and have an opportunity to do so. This is by being in an occupation that is essential to the survival of humans, such as farming, medicine, building houses, etc. They also can be working for the government or at the very least working for a company or individual. These companies or individuals either make a product or provide a service wanted by the public to increase their comfort level, happiness, or joy.

The economy is in the shape of a pyramid with the top being occupied by the rich with all the money, producing things for the masses, such as industrial goods and food, and at the same time controlling the money flow through banks and investment firms, living a life of luxury as we call it. They eat the best of food, own luxury homes, private planes, large yachts, and have the ability to travel anywhere in the world on a whim and save for their children and generations to come. This category may include some politicians too, who become such millionaires during their career but don't know how much salary they make.

At the bottom of the pyramid would be the blue-collar workers or the larger masses, such as factory workers and laborers, who spend their money to consume these products, living day-to-day life in rented apartments, possibly with some local holidays or travel, and owning a TV, fridge, and maybe a car.

The middle tier of the pyramid, of course, comprises white-collar workers. They also consume these products and are maybe able to save a few dollars for retirement or for their children and own a house to live by working for the government or in the service industry, such as the medical industry or in the engineering field. They will, of course, go on occasional overseas vacations too, but not at their whim. They will have to save for it as required.

So, we note that these blue-collar in the main and white-collar workers keep the economy going by consuming what the rich make, at the same time creating opportunities for their own survival as employment opportunities of varying degrees are of comfort for them too.

Chapter 10: Company

Summarizing what has been discussed in the previous chapter, a company means a group of people coming together and forming a legal entity to pool their money in order to manufacture a product or provide a service to the people. However, even a single person can start a company where he will be the sole owner. Mostly, it would be groups of people, as said before. A company may offer its shares, meaning part ownership of the company to raise money for its projects, if additional money is required. They are called shareholders. When profits are made, they all share the profit, and the value of the shares may increase. Similarly, when they lose money, the value of the shares may diminish.

The objective of every company is to make as much money as possible for its shareholders. As the desire to make more money increases, some may even flout the law or try to circumvent it to the point of breaking the law. It will not be a false statement, in my opinion, if it is to be stated that only a handful of companies would put the people's interest first rather than make more money in any possible way it can in the environment it operates. Even in the event of giving to charity, sometimes, it would be to enhance its reputation among the people, assuming such an image would make the people buy their products or at least will not object to their expansion even if this expansion would disrupt the environment.

The costliest item a company generally has is human labor, to which they must pay wages as well as offer many other benefits, such as holiday pay, medical insurance, etc. Hence, it is their will to always minimize the use of human labor. With the advent of technology, automation came to prominence, giving rise to machinery that could carry out repetitive tasks done by humans in factories.

When two or more companies market similar products, in order to be competitive, the companies will try to outsell the other by reducing the price. When the other matches this, it leads to a vicious cycle of possible tit-for-tat, leading to a reduction of their profit. Now, the shareholders may demand the company executives to increase or maintain the profit margin in whichever way possible, even to the extent of booting them out during shareholders' meetings if they fail. To this end, they would try cost-cutting wherever possible, and **Automation** (machinery doing repetitive human work) starts to look more appealing.

Mass-producing companies in the old days manufactured their products using assembly lines, where a mass of employees assembled the components of the product piece by piece in rows and rows. Now, machines would replace many such workers, saving the company payments in salary and benefits. By this, the masses may lose the opportunity for their livelihood or availability of jobs for them to make a living.

Sometimes, this is done to compete with the other companies who have automated their business already and hence to compete with them. Though some work opportunities are created in the companies involved in making these specialized pieces of machinery, the net consequence has been mass unemployment, disturbing the economic harmony of that society or even in the country. This was so witnessed by the introduction of the flying shuttle of the cotton wee-wee machine in the making of clothes, especially in England a long time ago. This devastated the economy of the British industry during that period by restricting the money going to the masses but a few. At the same time, it made that industry competitive against other countries who were still using direct labor methods to make the clothes or the handweaver, where the cotton plant grew, and labor was cheaper.

However, the issue here is not the few owners of such manufacturing companies making most of the money for themselves but the money not going to the masses as before. Due to this, their purchasing power is reduced. Therefore, unless the product was essential to the masses, they could not buy what these companies are producing when this happens on a large scale. This causes the economy to come to a somewhat standstill. Furthermore, these companies accumulating mass quantities of money make the economy more precarious sometimes by not investing this money back into the economy for new industries that produce new products for the masses as well as for export to other countries, bringing in foreign exchange.

These people would not reinvest their money again in the market due to various reasons, such as an uncertain political climate. This is where the company may think that a new government (Communist / Marxist / Socialist) may take over their factories due to the current high unemployment, where they, in turn, may also be culpable to an extent for this situation due to the introduction of automation in their factories as said before but inevitable in Capitalistic economy due to competition among industrialists to make the best profit possible to survive in the competitive market. Hence, there may be no money with the masses to purchase anything other than essential items, such as food. Therefore, the companies will be hanging onto whatever money they currently have without reinvesting it to make new products or upgrade their existing facilities.

There may also be other reasons for this to happen, such as false rumors about the future activities of the government, like a new regulation that the government is going to implement, which may be designed to curb inflation by restricting the supply of money to the hands of the people, reducing their purchasing power.

These situations have a spiraling effect on the economy. Now, the manufacturers of non-essential items would start cutting back on their production. This would lead to laying off factory workers. As they have no money now, they would not be buying any more non-essential stuff as before. So, in turn, these manufacturers would reduce their workforce further by going for more automation or shutting down existing production lines.

In the end, thc only people who would be having money to purchase non-essential items would be people working for the government and the few who are still working in the factories. Thus, we come to realize the importance of the type of government in power and their policies on the economy and the masses' perception of the policies of the government for the economic wellbeing of all its citizens. Now, the government, in order to improve this situation, may try to print more money and distribute it to the unemployed masses to purchase more products.

Hence, why the government or the so-called king in power cannot print more money and distribute it to the people when required to avoid such a situation is a valid question. Printing and freely distributing money would increase the purchasing power of the unemployed, and there would be a sustained demand for the goods and services again, leading at least to maintain the current employment rate for the masses. However, at the same time, the government would ensure that this distribution of money is not too much to discourage people from going to work. Throughout history, the government has been doing this from time to time by giving out unemployment benefits for the masses, leading to an increase in the national debt.

We will now consider what happens when the government does this. People get money to spend, which also goes with the confidence that more money would be coming from the government once they spend what they currently have. Now, people who normally spend frugally would start spending the free money lavishly. In addition, there would be a large amount of money circulating in the market called high **Liquidity,** as they spend. Hence, with this high liquidity, the demand for consumer goods will increase.

When this happens, the greedy manufacturers of these items put up the prices, knowing they could get higher prices for their products. This increase in prices would lead to a decrease in the purchasing power of the people at large, especially in categories of basic needs, such as food, clothing, etc. To compensate for this, the government would have to again increase the handouts to the people who are not working, reducing the value or the purchasing power of the money. In time, as said before, where it took $1.00 to buy a loaf of bread, it would now require $2.00. Notwithstanding this, the people who have gainful means of employment would demand more money from their employers or the government to compensate for this increase in prices, causing inflation.

Chapter 11: Inflation

Another interesting effect of this scenario is, by giving more printed money (notes) to the public, now they would have to carry a lot of notes to purchase their needs. The government would then add more zeros to the value of the currency notes they would be printing, as mentioned before. In the end, you would require counting notes in thousands just to buy a loaf of bread, making the purchasing power of the money of that country worthless.

This means millions would be required to buy a small car or billions to buy a house. Then one would wonder why the manufacturers and farmers are not increasing their production to cater to the higher demand and maintain the prices as before. There are three answers to this question in my view. One is that the factory output or farming output cannot be increased overnight as it takes time to install new machinery, find suitable land or source new raw material, etc. Most of all, the manufacturers or farmers would also want to reap the benefits of higher prices immediately than spend their capital on a long-term forecast.

Now, there is another twist to this situation. Most, if not all, countries import material, finished products, or food from other countries. There are various reasons for this, such as their climate not being suitable to grow a particular food item (example: sugarcane only grows in particular countries, and everyone uses sugar) or they do not have natural resources, such as rubber, aluminum, steel, etc. to make the product they require. Sometimes, even if they have the raw materials, they do not have the know-how for it, like the knowledge to make tires for the cars even though they have an abundance of rubber.

In this situation, for example, country A would import rare minerals from country B and make electronic products and sell the finished product back to country A or other countries. Both countries would pay each other in each other's currency too. For example, when country A imports from country B, country A pays country B in country B's currency and vice versa. To this effect, we would consider both these countries A & B have the other country's currency due to past trading, and each country takes the other country's currency as payment for its export to the other country.

Now say, for example, due to inflation in country B, the value of country B's currency gets diminished in relation to its purchasing power. This means country A would need more of country B's currency to import the same product and the same quantity than it paid earlier to country B. Meaning, in time, country B's currency that country A held would become worthless if this situation continues, especially if country B keeps on printing money to cover its expenditure over the income it receives from taxation, exports, etc. This is also because all the countries in the world cannot keep the currency of the other countries they trade with to pay for the goods it purchases. This brings to focus the need to have a universal mechanism or currency to pay for the trade of goods between countries.

Due to this, the exporting country A would now demand payment in US Dollars from other countries for their export, which it considers more stable in the open market. Now not only country A but most countries in the world, other than what we call the industrial countries, would demand payment in US Dollars. Now, we must understand that no country (except the US, which we will discuss later) can overprint money to give to the people in need above a limit. The world generally accepts this as a universal method for inter-country transactions. However, one country is now attempting to challenge this situation with their currency to replace the US dollar as this kingmaker.

Within a good economy, there is a balance between what the government takes from the employees and businesses and what it spends to maintain its bureaucracy, such as military, civil services, welfare payments to the needy, etc. However, when the economy turns bad, the tax collected by the government becomes less, and handouts expected by the needy go higher. This would force the government to either increase the tax on the workers and businesses or opt to print more money. The effect of printing more money seems to be different for the US than for the other countries as the other countries still accept the US Dollars as a method of payment for inter-country transactions, as mentioned before. For this, we need to understand the meaning of what underdeveloped, developing, and developed countries are.

Underdeveloped countries are countries that are poor, having a very low GDP (Gross Domestic Product) than most other countries of the world, with minimal industries and low substandard education and health systems. GDP means, in general, the ratio or the value of its industrial outputs and services in relation to its population. Developed countries are at the other end of the spectrum. They have stable economies and high GDP. Developing country GDP lies in between these two limits.

Developing countries are countries that are trying to manufacture products that had earlier been built or are still being built by developed countries at a lesser cost. For example, the US makes cars, but now Malaysia too wants to make cars and sell them to the US. As Malaysia's labor cost is cheaper, they could make cars at a much cheaper cost than the US. Also, to their benefit, the developed countries have a policy of open market. This is wherein underdeveloped or developing countries can sell competing products in that developed country without being subjected to discriminatory practices, such as targeted higher taxes on imported goods from those countries to the developed country unless the developed country considers these countries as an unfriendly country or a too strong competitor to its liking. Or this may be even another such developed country. In this situation, the developed country would impose very high taxation on these developing or underdeveloped country products coming to this developed country.

Sometimes, the items manufactured and produced by developed countries become unsellable in their own country due to higher unemployment, possibly because of economic conditions gone wrong. In such times, a developing or underdeveloped country would create more jobs for its people by increasing its sales of somewhat comparative lower quality products to the developed country, which, of course, would be cheaper than the same product made in that developed country and accumulate more of the US dollars for its reserves for its own purchases from other countries.

For example, in the US, when the economy goes bad, more people flock to dollar shops, where everything sold is around one dollar and comes mainly from developing or underdeveloped countries, even if their quality does not match that of the same product made in the US. This would cause the economy of such exporting country to improve, but the developed country's economy to become worse.

Now, the only recourse available to the developed country is to develop similar products with better quality which would be in demand by the world even at a higher price or at least near the same cost of the same product sold by a developing country. The latter would be difficult if not for the application of automation wherever possible. This means the developed country will always have to be more innovative to make better products than others as well as to cut the cost of manufacturing all the time to maintain its economic standing and product competitiveness in the world. Not an easy task.

Sometimes, developed countries find other means to maintain their status as developed countries. This is by creating civil unrest or wars in other countries in order to sell arms to these countries. Such industries in developed countries are of large scale with many employers and employees. Furthermore, developed countries would demand payment for goods it sells to a developing country in its own currency, US dollar, or in gold.

This would cause the developing country to sell products to the developed country in order to earn the currency of the developed country. This situation gives the developed country the upper hand to purchase what it wants selectively at a price the developed country dictates. Now, if the developing country does not have an acceptable currency that the developed country wants, the developed country may even demand payment in gold, which is another universal currency due to its characteristics, which we discussed earlier.

One might argue as to why the developing country would want anything from the developed country than making of their own as much as possible and live within their means. The answer to this lies in their need to meet the demands of its people who request fancy items to satisfy their egos. These can be categorized as cars and white goods, such as fridges or washing machines, the developed country makes, etc. This, in addition, is to keep its military the strongest due to possible war situations created with its neighbors or even spread its religious dogma to its neighbors by force. This would provide an opportunity for the developed country to sell its arms to the developing country, which may have the resources the developed country wants. Then there are situations like the need for the developing country to acquire cutting-edge medical devices etc., as shown by the recent clamor for COVID-related products from the developed countries, which the developed countries have manufactured. Or even food in emergency situations.

For example, country X in the Middle East has the vast oil wealth that a developed country wants. Country X needs to have a strong military to keep its neighbors under control so that they obey its orders. This the developed country does not mind because it considers country X as its friend. Now, the developed country would sell its advance military equipment to country X for its oil wealth and keep its economy humming. Now everyone would be happy other than the poor countries around country X. If country X now becomes unfriendly, then the developed country will give more arms to another country near country X to topple country X's rulers and bring in friendly rulers back to power.

Occasionally, developed countries even try to maintain their economies by increasing their populations by allowing new immigrants to come in each year. This is in the expectation that they would bring in some money to buy cars, houses, fridges, etc., increasing the demand for such products or at the least maintain such demands in the service and manufacturing sector, sustaining or growing their economies.

However, this policy is a double-edged sword. In time, the people who are immigrating would demand similar or better jobs than even the existing people of the country based on being better educated than this country's own people due to the fear of being marginalized in this new country. The people of this country may be more complacent, thinking this is my country than becoming more competitive for achievements than the immigrants. In time, even the prior occupants of these countries would start working for these new immigrants who might even take control of the economy, as history has shown as happed in some developed countries.

Therefore, the countries that do this have to allow people to immigrate to the country continuously every year to maintain or increase the purchasing power of its people to maintain its economy if there is no other alternative to keep the economy going.

Another method used by developed countries is to sell their products and maintain the employment of their people by forming open market treaties. In this scenario, a developed country would import raw materials from a developing or underdeveloped country on preferential treatment, such as low taxes, and expect the underdeveloped country to buy its products in return. In other words, the developed country would increase the number of consumers for the products it makes, thereby minimizing unemployment. However, the underdeveloped country might start its own industry and compete with the developed country in time. This will cause unemployment in the developed country if it fails to produce more innovative products than the underdeveloped country. Therefore, this would be a temporary fix for the developed country.

None of the countries that trade with other countries is allowed to print money without a limit. The only country in the world that is somewhat doing this is the USA, called the ultimate banker. This is because all the countries accept the US Dollar for their trading with other countries. The USA can back the value of the Dollar due to large quantities of raw materials, energy products, or even gold and silver that they have to produce vast quantities of commercial and agricultural products. On the other hand, the military strength it has is enough to justify intervention in any country, except a few, at any given time and call it justified. In other words, as the saying goes, ‘he who has the biggest gun is always right and just.’ Couple these together, the USA is a mighty force indeed to back up its currency unit, the Dollar.

To this end, the people of the USA tend to consume more resources than any other country in the world, where a part of it comes from imports. This gives a market for other countries to sell their products to the USA. In return, this creates a demand for the products of other countries and ensures employment or means of existence to the people in those countries. When more dollars are required, the USA would print more of the same and say ‘I owe myself’ so much and ironically even give interest on what it owes to itself.

Hence, the countries that export to the USA hoard or spend the acquired US Dollars to purchase more machinery, arms, or other agricultural products from other countries. This can bring about trade agreements where a developed country would demand other countries to buy goods only from their country, or it would cease its purchases from these other countries. In turn, the developed country would dictate its own prices for the raw materials from the developing or underdeveloped country. Sadly, this is how developed countries tend to monopolize world trade at the expense of poor countries, depriving a fair price for their resources.

Another thing we must keep in mind is the problem of localization of wealth among a limited number of people who may be industrialists or bankers etc. Here, we can define wealth as paper money and fixed assets as land or buildings. The buildings constitute cement, bricks, glass, etc. It seems interesting that even if these people do not reinvest this wealth, maybe due to uncertainty in the economy, nature seems to have a way to even things out apart from inflation. This would include things like death, decay, sickness, natural calamity as tsunamis, earthquakes, or cyclones, where these natural phenomena will destroy this accumulated wealth and mostly would make this wealth unavailable or useless to that person with death or an incurable disease, such as terminal cancer.

We will now consider the situation of paper money accumulation or non-invested money and inflation. As mentioned before, inflation takes place when the government is forced to print more money than it gets from taxing people. This can be a tax on a person's wages, food purchases, property, even if that person is not employed, or death tax on a person's holdings, even if the person is now DEAD.

As stated before, inflation is when the government prints more money to hand out to the unemployed or when it starts new megaprojects to keep people employed, and where the government earnings from tax are not sufficient to pay for this expenditure. When this happens, the price of goods goes up as the greedy manufacturers increase their product prices, knowing there would now be a higher demand for goods and services. Hence, as stated before, the purchasing power of money decreases. For example, a person who has saved 1 million dollars in his bank account could have previously bought 10 tons of food items for his village, whereas after one year, with say 10% inflation, it may be near to 9 tons only he could buy assuming he buys only now with this one million. Similarly, next year it may only be near to 82 tons at the same inflation rate. The point here is, if money is not properly invested by anyone, with time, they would only have just paper in the bank.

Let us condense what we have talked about so far. Firstly, the economy is the structure that is put in place by the government to effectively facilitate all the citizens to have an opportunity to earn a living. This facilitation may be in the form of laws and regulations. These laws and regulations will have a profound effect on the economy positively or negatively, depending on how these laws are formulated and where and how they are meant to be effective.

For instance, the government may declare that people with higher income would have to pay higher taxes, and this would dampen the economic activity. The entrepreneurs or the businesspersons would be hesitant to make new investments or take risks because earning over a certain limit will only bring in lesser profit as they would have to pay a larger share of their hard-earned money to the government. However, if he loses his investment, the government will not give back his money even though the investor may only be able to recover part of the loss from the tax they owe to the government from a profitable part of the business if they have such. To this end, these people may consider it is better to keep the money in the bank than reinvest it in the economy.

However, as discussed before, this money sitting in a bank will only generate an extremely low interest or none. The net effect of this is the money would not be circulating nor be available for new product development that would normally have generated opportunities for the others to earn a share of this. On the other hand, if there are no regulations, most rich would very much try to swindle the money of the masses by activities, such as Ponzi schemes, or even cause an artificial increase in prices.

Therefore, no regulations or too many regulations, both are detrimental to the economy, and such an environment does not uplift the living standards of the ordinary masses. Furthermore, this does not contribute to real economic activity as the development of new products, innovations, etc. which now become constrained. This situation also sucks out the buying power of the masses to a few individuals that block the money going back to the economy. Thus, the correct balanced application of these laws and regulations bears a profound effect on the success or the failure of the economy.

Now we see different government policies in this regard to uplift the economic situation of the masses in their society, which they think is the correct approach. These approaches can be categorized as **Capitalist** or **Socialist,** coming under a **Democratic** rule or **Marxism** / **Communism** / **Fascism** under **Dictatorial** rule.

Chapter 12: Organization or Society

A long time ago, the countries were ruled by kings and queens who were termed as rulers. As mentioned before, in some instances, the ruler imposed higher taxes due to situations, such as war, to pay for newly recruited soldiers or even when his tax income went down due to natural reasons like bad weather, etc. This sometimes led to resentment among his subjects, where the ruler or government got overthrown. A new ruler would then take his place, promising the subjects better economic benefits. However, if things did not improve, the new ruler may even get thrown out, imprisoned, or beheaded in some instances.

As society progresses, the king or queen in power would hope that they would not be beheaded or imprisoned. Therefore, they may instruct their subjects to govern by themselves, and the king or queen would only act as their leader with powers to intervene if it is required, still keeping with them all the benefits such position entails. When things go wrong, the ruler can now blame the people who ran the government and keep his or her head intact.

Even so, sometimes, when the economy goes through bad situations, the people would still wish to get rid of the king or queen to save on their tax payments, blaming the ruler for the bad economy and maybe focusing on the high expenses it takes to keep that ruler in power. When this is applied to present times, it is called **Cost-Cutting**, and this may have been the first instance of its use. With the right to govern given to the people, and the economy going wrong, there would be many people who would claim to know how to fix the economy or make it 100% for the masses again.

As said before, at one extreme, this is described as capitalism, an economic system that allows people the freedom of selecting someone to govern them, someone they believe could get the job done. At the other end is communism or Marxism, another economic system that promotes dictatorship, meaning only a privileged few would always govern, and the masses have no choice in the matter.

Under the democratic rule, people have elections and vote for different parties to bring them to power. This is to make the economy 100% as per their beliefs and principles they hold. People create political parties under this democracy. These parties put forward different ideas to steer the economy. At specific periods, they visit the people and ask for their vote to be elected to the country's governing body. We will not dwell too much on this as we all know how this works differently from country to country. They still follow the same basic principles of people voting them to power after a particular period.

However, it is noted that the selection process through which a party comes in power does not only come from people due to economic conditions but also the prevailing economic policies. Nevertheless, this is sometimes due to an embedded belief that a specific party is for the benefit of the poor or best for the economy, irrespective of what may happen to the economy under the policies of that party.

The opportunity for people to make a living by their own business or working for others tapers off as the economy becomes stagnant. Meaning, there is no development of new products for the people wishing to buy or use them to better their lives, for the enjoyment of the masses, or for any other reason. They must purchase standard items, such as the same food or clothing for survival.

Now people get agitated against whoever is in control of the government, be it a king, president, prime minister, or any other person, under any of the systems when the economy goes bad. Furthermore, with the advent of the industrial revolution, meaning machines doing the work of some people, few manufacturers became richer at the expense of many workers that we call the masses. They are the government workers, service workers, etc. The ordinary masses, who are the majority, become envious and angry of these rich people, especially when they are suffering, and the rich seem to be having a good time.

As unemployment increases, the unemployed, in desperation, would seek work for lesser pay than the current rate enjoyed by their compatriots currently in employment. Under this scenario, the rich would know that there is an ample supply of cheap labor. Taking advantage of this situation, some employers, especially in capitalist systems, would demand higher productivity from their employees for the same pay, or, if possible, lesser pay now.

Under these circumstances, the employers may force the ordinary workers to work additional hours for the same pay, knowing that the employees have no option available in this regard. In some instances, the employers would give a little back to the masses or society as a charity, but many times with an ulterior motive of gaining the goodwill of the masses in order to sell more of their products against competitors. In the end, the poor will always look at the rich as the enemy.

However, when such situations happen, the masses get angry with the rich and subsequently with the government in control. If the situation is further compounded by a sudden imbalance in the economy, which may be due to natural calamities, the government in power may try to stay in power by competing with the opposition. The opposition would now promise the masses a better economy by offering free handouts if they come to power or, in the worst scenario, take ownership of everything the rich has. This, in the short run, may work, but in the long term, it would make the economy worse. It would be so bad that the masses would now want to try out extremes in this regard, like communism or Marxism or even under dictatorship, by revolting against the current government. Where on paper, socialism should be the preferred option as it says sharing the wealth by all equally.

The fundamental fact we tend to forget is that all individuals are capitalist by nature. Only about 0.000000001% or even less would be true socialists who will share their wealth with others and endeavor to make more wealth, and consequently, drive the economy or the living standards of all one notch higher, creating more employment opportunities for the people of the society and more riches for themselves either through increased self-esteem or inner peace via one's humanitarian achievements.

A good example of this, to my knowledge, is the Bill Gates family and maybe very few other unsung who we call Billionaires. They spent many billions of dollars of their money for medical research (more employment for researchers, assistant researchers, office personal, etc.), i.e., putting that money back into society by creating new employment opportunities for the masses and, at the same time, coming out with new products that the people wish to purchase locally as well as internationally, leading to more or sustained employment in the USA. This also provides the government with higher tax revenues in varied ways, such as income tax from employees, value-added tax from products sold, etc. All this contributes to a good economy for the masses.

Alternatively, an example would be someone spending large amounts of money to create a revolution in another country, to bring the people of their choice to power, so they could purchase raw materials available in that country at a bargain price. This tends to create higher employment in the country the revolution was organized in. This is due to the lower cost of finished goods and availability of more competitive products in the market against imported products, creating a higher quality of life for the people of that country. At the least, this would guarantee the availability of raw materials to the people of the country who organize this type of revaluation. A case in point in this regard is the bloody revolutions caused in some African countries to possess their diamond and gold mines some years back.

Now, if the same raw material is available in both a developed country and a developing country, the developed country would still try to obtain this cheaper from the developing country rather than use the higher-priced material already available in the developed country. This is to conserve their raw material for future use and because of the higher cost involved in extracting it from one's own country due to labor costs that is invariably higher. Sometimes, this could be to avoid causing damage to one's own environment, such as polluting the water supply in this process, but most often than not, having utter disregard to the developing country's environment.

Nevertheless, sometimes the government of that developed country may determine that such imports of raw material would lead to unemployment in their own country as the mining and material-processing jobs will tend to disappear. Notwithstanding that, in an emergency, the immediate availability to process raw materials for impending wars, etc., will not be possible if such raw materials are not available in one's own country when needed immediately.

Importation of raw materials would also increase the trade deficit of the developed country against its trading partners. In order to strike a balance, the developed country would impose a tariff on selected imported items. This would become a special tax the importer of this raw material must pay the government, increasing the price of the said raw materials. This would now discourage the developed country from purchasing this raw material from other countries. Hence, on occasion, it is considered as an exception to the basics of capitalism and the notion of free trade among all its trading partners. The point here is, there are no fixed boundaries between all the different ways of managing the economy. Be it capitalism, socialism, or communism, the boundaries between them are sometimes somewhat blurred.

On the other hand, the country which has this raw material can sell this product to another developed country at a lesser fixed price due to a special trade agreement between the two countries done by a prior government. In this situation, the first country would be at a great disadvantage in having to sell its products at a lower price when the world demand has increased. Now, if the first country is socialist and has less military power and refuses to sell this product to the developed country at these low prices and demand a higher price, they may face the consequences, such as the government being toppled in order to have a government favorable to the developed country. So, we see there are other forces that can act against the economy of a country other than capitalism or communism, as discussed earlier.

In the end, the poor will always look at the rich as the enemy. Therefore, from time to time, people overthrow their governments ruled by either a king or president or opt for another form of the economic system than the existing one. For example, the economic system may shift from capitalism to socialism or from socialism to capitalism, or even to Marxism or communism.

Chapter 13: Marxism, Communism, or Dictatorship

Under communist rule, any multi-party system promoters would get abolished through imprisonment, expelled from the country, or even made to disappear. These people, known as Marxists, communists, or dictators, are not the majority but somehow in power by some means and see political parties as a burden on society. They think that the best way to make the economy 100% is out of the barrel of a gun. Regretfully, they forget that more than 99 % of us in society are all capitalists. Meaning, none of us would do anything for others if there were no benefits for us in doing so. Meaning for one to consider helping others, they want to be economically sound first. Then, of course, there is the exception of that 1% or less.

The minority Marxist or communist would get power mostly through a revolution, while most of the masses look on. Although they are protesting the rich, they would discretely enjoy the wealth by themselves or with their party members while the masses suffer once they achieve power. The masses would subsequently have no say in the matters related to governing or on economic decisions.

Also, in Marxism or communism, there is no incentive for the people to be innovative or take risks in order to accumulate more wealth. This is because everything is owned by the government, even to the extent of the lives of the people. Thus, everyone would be working for the government one way or the other. In the name of equitable distribution of wealth, the government even decides the occupation one should engage in, such as a doctor or engineer or farmer, or even laborer. History has shown that this type of government would not sustain itself and would collapse once the wealth accumulated by a previous capitalist or even a socialist government is exhausted.

However, a selected few may now enjoy the fruits of the hard labor of the masses who may call them the governing body or the people's congress, etc., for eternity. Unfortunately, to become a member of such a group, you must become a member of the sole existing party. This means a billion or more people's lives would be determined by a few thousand enjoying all the benefits.

However, now you may not call them 'Sir' as in a capitalist society, implying a higher rank, but 'Comrade' implying equality. Nevertheless, the punishment would be severe if you dared to disobey the direction of a superior comrade. Then, of course, there is also less recourse to justice than in a capitalist system unless one has a close alliance with a higher-ranking party member. Also, there would be no media that would dare to criticize the party as they too may disappear.

Chapter 14: Capitalism

Capitalism is having laws enacted by the government, which gives the people vast liberties to benefit from one's entrepreneurship. Risk-taking, innovativeness, hard work can be stated as the essential attributes to having a good economy that could drive it one notch at a time to sustain and enhance every one economic situation. This provides opportunities for anyone to make money. However, people will take advantage of this situation by going to any extreme to make money by unethical behavior, getting what they want "by hook or crook," as the saying goes, if allowed to do so.

Unfortunately, even if there were a few who would stick by the rules, the devastation created by such unscrupulous capitalistic people would destroy the concept of genuine capitalism. Such organizations are the ones that try to profit by speculations at the expense of others. They drive the economy sometimes to be like a building with a weak foundation that collapses with the slightest disturbance. This was clearly visible in the past, with mortgage lenders giving credit to people to buy houses when they do not have a good financial foundation to make large mortgage payments. This was evident by the last housing market crash in the USA.

We can additionally see that those people had even lost their deposits when they were evicted out of their houses by mortgage lenders when they defaulted in their monthly mortgage payments. This was when the economy fell, and they lost their jobs, and they were unable to pay the large monthly payments that were required. This was also due to the additional premium they had to pay if they could not put down 20% of the mortgage amount. So mortgage companies still give mortgages with a higher additional monthly charge for lesser deposit payments, say 10% or even 5% down, enticing people who were barely able to pay the mortgage.

Had they been in an apartment during the bad economic times with less rent to pay, they could have waited until the economy improved saved more money for a 20% deposit for a less monthly mortgage payment, which they could possibly have managed even during the bad times. In essence, people who could barely offer monthly payments got enticed and suckered by large mortgage companies and, in the end, lost even the 10% or 5% deposit when mortgage companies ceased the houses. And not only that, the capital they had paid too.

For example, say someone buys a house for 200,000 dollars with 10% down, which is 20,000 excluding other fees charged by the mortgage company. This is without any reserve after scratching the barrel due to the enticements by the mortgage companies of owning your own home, in the end, owing 180,000 to the bank as the mortgage. Then another 100 dollars a month to the bank as mortgage insurance as they only could pay 10% and not the required 20% down with a further 5,000 per year in taxes. Now, every month they barely manage to pay 250 dollars of the principal and the interest, which we would say is another 750 dollars. Say in two years (24 months), they would have paid in all nearly 20,000 + (5,000*2) ((100+250+750)*24) = 56,400 dollars when the breadwinner loses their job and cannot pay any more monthly payments. The mortgage company now puts the house in the open market for auction after the eviction of the owners. The price of the house has gone up in the open market to say 210,000 or 5% in two years, which could normally be the case. Now, someone close to the mortgage company will bid for this house and get it for, say 180,000, which is the money owed to the bank. Then he does some renovation, say for 5,000, and sells it back in the market for 210,000. Now, in all, the original buyer has lost nearly 56,400 – (1000*24) = 32,400 dollars, and the vultures would have made a good profit. The 1000*24 is what they could have paid if they were in an apartment during this time. This is capitalism at the worst.

The best way to understand how capitalism works is to consider the political parties in the USA, which are considered the most capitalist in the world. There are two main parties in the USA considered as an economic success story by all other countries or at least by most of the world. They are the **Democratic Party** and the **Republican Party**. Less common are the Liberals or the Libertarians. The Democratic Party principles are to the left of the spectrum of capitalism, which means increasing the size of the government to increase the economy and to have higher laws and regulations controlling the big businesses and more stringent environmental laws etc. The Republican Party viewpoints are more to the right of the spectrum as they believe in less government (fewer taxes to maintain government). They give more liberty to big businesses and have fewer environmental rules that permit further exploitation of the natural resources in order to improve employment and more profits by the big businesses.

In between sits the liberals in the said spectrum, supporting environmental protections as the Democrats do and believe in the free-market economy as the Republicans. Now, a question comes to mind as to how the economy could be deemed great in this country with all these divergent views. To this, the answer lies in the fact that if you consider the entire spectrum of policies of all these parties, they still do not move much from the central idea of free-market economic activity. Hence, the core ideas remain the same, with some deviations in the fringes up to now.

Chapter 15: Socialism

Socialism is an attempt to strike a balance between the two extremes of economies we mentioned before, capitalism and communism / Marxism / dictatorship. In socialism, while encouraging capitalistic economic growth, the government would try to influence or directly intervene to spread the wealth to the masses in general by different types of taxes, such as death tax, income tax, capital gains tax, etc. where these tax gets redistributed as medical benefits and handouts to the poor. It is observed that the poor people, in turn, would spend 100% of this money to purchase their basic needs. This money thus gets rolled back to the rich, who are producers of the needs of the people or the service providers.

From history, we have seen that societies have been experimenting with different types of economies and switching from one to the other, depending on their success or lack of it.

It is the view of the author that for an economic policy to be good, it needs to have certain fundamental features. The most important of these are the laws of the society that nurture prime movers or entrepreneurs; for example, the type of farsighted risk-taking visionaries like Howard Hughes, Henry Ford, and now Elon Musk, or even Bill Gates and maybe others. They carried the whole society by increasing the standard of living of the masses one notch at a time by their vision of the future and entrepreneurship.

As per the government policies, it minimizes taxes on reinvestment, research and development, and other capital projects, ensuring the wealth accumulated is reinvested back to society. These activities, in turn, provide jobs or opportunities for the masses to earn a living. To this end, in no instance should the government takeover assets of the prime movers, increase taxes unduly, or put laws restricting company activities other than when it really affects the environment.

However, it is also necessary to ensure that companies do not monopolize different business sectors in order to make unreasonable profits by encouraging competition from other vendors that make the same product at the same time. Furthermore, to ensure they do not destroy the environment by felling trees without replacements, polluting water and air, etc., in pursuit of making more money.

Another requirement is the need to have an education policy for a pool of educated personnel at different levels of education to assist the said prime movers in bringing their vision to reality. This is possible by developing their ideas at the Ph.D. level, making the factory run smoothly at the BS level, helping in the assembling of products by studying instructions learned at the high school level, and cleaning jobs at the middle to no school level.

This may, of course, sound very cruel, but if every person were a Ph.D., BS, or MBA and demanded the same status and salary, then there would be no people to do the menial work. There will always be thousands of menial workers available apart from the research and management level. However, in a just society, the comfort level between the Ph.D. and MBA to menial level is narrowed as much as possible, with the menial level too enjoying some aspects of basic riches like a car, TV, occasional holiday, etc. They would enjoy the occasional holiday while the extraordinarily rich class would, of course, have the luxury of frequent holidays at will or purchase things considered pleasurable, such as yachts and private planes, jewelry, and clothing to fulfill their egos.

Even if one assumes that the economy is at a perfect level with opportunities for everyone to enjoy the necessities for existence with the prime movers satisfying their ego by utilizing more money than they could easily use in a personal capacity, nature sometimes tends to put a spanner in the works.

Chapter 16: Big-Ticketing Items Affecting the Economy

Housing:

In this scenario, the importance of housing is tremendous as it affects every single person. Thus, the entropy (degree of contribution) is extreme. The importance here is the need to keep on increasing the quality of the housing continuously to maintain them. As such, the people would be spending their income on materials, like bricks, wood, appliances, cement, sand, plants, and paint, making an avenue to put that money into the economy for others to pick up continuously for many years, like 15-30, during their lifetime. No other aspect of human activity generates such a wide degree of positive effects to the economy continuously for such long periods as houses do, as said including subsequent modifications and repairs, contributing to the purchase of these related hardware items continuously, not to mention the employment provided to many millions of carpenters, electricians, plumbers, roofers, handyman, etc. during this period.

Entertainment:

Entertainment can be considered a large contributor to the economy also. Unlike housing, where everybody needs a place to live, a smaller number of people may be involved in entertainment at any given time. The degree of contribution is also less as the money spent mostly goes to few people, such as the artist, and not spread widely among society. As in this situation, the material purchases are mostly limited to making CDs, buying musical instruments, TVs, and going to cinemas. The entropy of monetary value may not exceed an average of hundred dollars per month. As an example, if a household of four spends a guaranteed amount of $1000 on their mortgage, the entertainment contribution would only range from nothing to a few hundred dollars.

Vehicles:

Similar can be said about vehicles that the poor purchase as the life of these vehicles may be lower than the ones purchased by the rich. Subsequently, the vehicles would break down, and the poor would spend more money to fix them. As for the rich, they would buy better quality new vehicles lasting for a long time. At the same time, the rich may sell that car soon and buy a better new car. The point here is, the rich now enjoys the good car and recover some of the money spent by selling it. On the other hand, the poor who buy this used car or a lesser quality car will use it for some time until it breaks down and subsequently throw it as scrap if it is too expensive to repair. By this, the poor would lose all the money they spent on the car. It is particularly important to understand this phenomenon.

The money spent by such people just vanishes into thin air by the deterioration of the product, such as metal, plastic, rubber, used to make the object, which in this case is a car. Due to the poor now having to spend money to repair the car at a garage, some of this money will manifest in the hands of the ordinary masses, such as mechanics, contributing to the sustenance of the ordinary people or to the people who make these spare parts. The rich would spend less or none to purchase parts for their cars as they are new, while the poor continuously spend on buying parts for their old cars if they could and then to the junkyard as scrap metal. With cars coming to the market in millions each year, this too has a profound effect, as said before, on the health of the economy.

Health Care:

Another important contributor to the economy is the field of health care. Though we wish none of us would get sick with no requirement for medicines or doctors, this is not the reality. Every year, millions of us get sick, and we consume millions of rupees worth of drugs. Additionally, more money would be spent to get the required diagnostic reports, such as X-Rays or Cat-Scans. This provides employment to thousands of people, such as doctors, nurses, laboratory technicians, attendants, janitors, people who produce drugs, and people who run the medical insurance companies, keeping that money flowing from one person to the other to sustain the economy. Some economists also say that a significant part of the economy is based on the health industry.

Food:

Growing food is an important contributor to the economy that keeps us alive. However, with one person growing food for many thousands of people using machinery, the direct economic impact for employment for others has become less profound. The money earned from such farming circulates only around a handful of individuals. We also need to keep in mind that these large-scale farmers now must pay a lot of money to acquire farming machinery and maintain it. The price of food in the market is subject to fluctuations, to such an extent that farmers may even lose money in the end. Sometimes, the price they can sell their produce may be lower than the investment made to grow it due to the glut of it in the market from many producers or importers of these food items. This is not to mention what happens due to drought, flooding, etc. Another facet to this is that in the food production industry, there is a need to process and transport it to the masses in the cities and store it until purchased by the consumer. This creates many employment opportunities for ordinary people, like food processors, workers, supermarket employees, and the transporters, such as drivers.

Transportation:

This, too, is an important activity to sustain the economy. Here, people would spend their money at a reasonably high value for air travel to go from one place to another for business, to visit relatives, or for holidays. In doing so, they spend their money on hoteling, shopping for gifts, conveyance, etc., to name a few. It has been estimated that millions of people travel by air and train during holidays in the United States, India, and China, as well as many other countries. All this money now goes to the economy for others to benefit from, including the airline owners, who are, however, few in numbers.

Religion:

How does religion, which we will discuss in detail later, affect or contribute to the economy? Consider some great religious leaders commanding their followers to give 2.5% of their wealth to the needy every year to get good graces from their God or to get more money than they give. If this were true, in say 50 years of that person's life, approximately most of his or her money or wealth would be redistributed back to the poor masses. This would improve their economy or help the poor to purchase the basics for sustenance. Furthermore, all the other religions advocate charity to the needy. This may be in cash distributions, food, or other charitable ways. This helps the economy of the poor masses, enabling them to purchase food for their basic sustenance. This money, of course, will now get back to the givers again as they would be the producers of these basic items as industrialists, vendors or farmers, etc., keeping the economic cycle going to benefit all.

Wars:

Wars have pulled many economies out of the woods many times. A great example of this is the economy of the USA. World War II assisted the USA in recovering from the Great Depression. How does this happen? Sometimes when there is a war, the government starts spending vast amounts of money to make military equipment. This money filters to the masses through additional job creation, enabling them to purchase their daily requirements. However, it is noteworthy that this situation is especially applicable to the USA. We had discussed this earlier as to why mainly only the USA could do this and maybe few other developed countries with vast resources. These governments can print money without substantially reducing the value of their currency. This is especially true in the USA, as mentioned before. Furthermore, the opposition parties would support the ruling party so during wartimes, as they do not want to be called traitors to their country.

Nature:

Nature has important aspects related to the above. In most of these cases, the products we buy come from the elements of the environment. This may be synthesized, formed, or molded to make products that sustain us or enhance our ego. However, with time, these products would decay, giving an opportunity for the manufacturers of these products to make more of the same and maintain its demand for the future. For example, we will take the case of a building. Even a brand-new building made from bricks, iron, wood, etc., would in time decay or rust due to various weather conditions. It will perish with time or be destroyed by natural disasters, such as tornados, cyclones, floods, or even tsunamis, which we call acts of God or nature. Then, there would be famine due to sudden lack of rain, the spread of insects destroying the crops, tsunami, volcanic eruptions, etc. So, we see there is quite a handful of ways for nature to do this.

Now, we will consider what happens when a wealthy owner dies of natural causes. This wealth mostly gets distributed to more people as family inheritance, and they would release this money back to the economy through purchases or bank it. They may also wisely reinvest this money into the economy and make more money. With time, if the ones that hoarded the money in a bank dies, the wealth is again redistributed among their offspring, and even sometimes it would be confiscated by the government, especially if there is no will by the deceased. This money also most often would get devalued due to inflation as it has not been invested to increase its value. Hence, even if one person hoards a vast amount of money, with time, it will be distributed to the economy, or its value or purchasing power will eventually deplete.

Then there are disasters, as said, such as tsunamis, earthquakes, cyclones, and wildfires, etc., that occur in this world. This causes the insurance companies and the governments to spend billions of monies on assisting the people in rebuilding property lost. Now such affected people would purchase building material and even their lost personal items, from clothes to furniture and fridges, carpets, cookers, etc., putting money back to the economy. This money otherwise gets stored somewhere and would only benefit the shareholders of the insurance companies who are few against the vast number of people benefiting from this now. Certainly, we do not wish this to happen despite it helping the economy in a positive way. Then, needless to say, regretfully, all the people would not have an insurance policy to cover such a situation, and no government handouts are sufficient in these situations to fully cover one's losses.

In addition, there comes a time on the horizon when the market demand for certain products starts waning as the public enthusiasm saturates, or one may lose interest in this product. This is part of our nature. This product demand saturation profoundly calls for a newer or better product to sustain the initial interest of the public. Therefore, the need arises for Research & Development (R&D) to enhance the existing products or to make new products with different features to tempt the masses to purchase them in order to sustain the economic development.

Research & Development (R&D) and Science:

With the scope of increasing the comfort level of humanity by one notch, science too plays a crucial part in research and development. It provides new material and new ways to make better products where the masses would discontinue using the current product and buy the new product. This distributes the money to the economy. Similarly, new discoveries, such as the invention of televisions, electricity, etc., compel the population to spend their money to increase the quality of life by another notch.

Unlike other aspects discussed above, there is a long lead-time for the effects of R&D to contribute to the economy. However, this makes a vital contribution to the sustenance of the economy in the end.

Customs, Festivals, and Celebrations:

Almost every society in this world has different customs related to their religion or nationality. For example, the western world celebrates Mother's Day, Father's Day, Valentine's Day, and Christmas, to say a few. In all these scenarios, people buy different products, which may vary from food items, gifts, decorative items, etc. If it is food or drinks, it will exceed normal consumption. As an example, people may purchase chocolates or alcohol that might not be consumed regularly. In other words, there would also be a hike in the consumption of meat, alcohol, etc. All these customs or events provide the vendors and their staff an opportunity to earn a living or contribute to the economy.

Electronic Gadgets

A few years back, microwaves, fridges, washing machines, mobile phones, TVs, computers, electronic game consoles, or similar items were non-existent. Now, with the advent of the electronic era, we have access to them every day. In a recent visit to a recycling center, I was amazed to see the number of such items being discarded by people. This means they continuously replace these items with better models bearing more features or functionality. This, in turn, means a large workforce of people working in these factories can make a living. So much so that some countries, such as Japan, Korea, and China, are greatly sustaining their economies by making these devices. Not to mention, these electronic games are highly popular among the young and even some adults—an industry in its own right.

We have now seen some key aspects that help to grow or at least sustain our economy. However, for these aspects to help grow an economy, someone would have to take the initiative. For example, for a scientist to discover the transistor, an essential item in all our electronic gadgets, someone or an organization has to encourage or facilitate the scientist or entrepreneur to this end with its leadership or guidance. For example, if it is a university, it would be the leadership of the lead scientist or professor of that subject or department that would be providing the technical leadership. Above that would be the vice-chancellor of the university, who would provide the funding or financial leadership or policy leadership for the relevant research to proceed. Finally, it would be the government or philanthropist that would provide the ultimate leadership by providing billions of taxpayers' money to the universities to this end. The leadership of the government would be as per their own beliefs; for instance, how the economy should be run and, in this case, what assistance the university should avail on its own to this end. For example, the government may give billions of monies to the universities to do research in cutting-edge military technology. However, in a capitalistic society, this leadership may even come from private organizations.

Chapter 17: Leadership

Earlier, we talked about different kinds of governments affecting the economy, such as capitalism, communism, and socialism. Out of these, we saw that the most effective government with the ability to provide the masses a way to earn a livelihood was capitalism. Under this system, the people at the bottom end would not be enjoying a much comfortable life while the high-end people enjoy most of the benefits. In other words, the wealth of the land is not justly distributed.

Note here that we are not saying that the distribution of wealth to the risk-takers or the wealth generators should not be more than those at the bottom end in a capitalistic society. However, it would be morally unjust not to provide a good standard of living to upkeep the bottom-end people or the poor, as they are the ones who sustain the risk-takers by consuming their products.

In reality, some of the risk-takers, if given the opportunity, would squeeze the last drop from the bottom-end people, and this is the extreme nature of capitalism. This would not be good for the economy as the wealth then tends to be localized and not spread to sustain the continuity of the economy. Now, the leadership of a capitalist society, such as the president or prime minister, would ensure such practices do not take place whilst also protecting the risk-takers from undue penalization by distributing their wealth through higher taxations. Having such a leader is considered pivotal in an economy, as their policies would sustain a good economy for all the members of the society.

In general, economic leadership comes from the highest level of the government from the laws they enact or do not enact for any economy to flourish. In general, the more laws the government introduces related to the economy, the less would be the economic vitality of that country. At the same token, fewer rules would make the bottom end of the society venerable to exploitation by the rich. So, a good leader can be someone or a policymaker who has the knack for a balanced approach to this. Here, our focus was economic leadership and not, for example, leadership in a battle or war. However, ultimate leadership is the economic leadership that matters in the end. In this regard, a wise leader would anticipate the effect of upcoming technological developments to take advantage of such or mitigate any pending adverse effects of such on the economy as during the advent of the computer in the 20th century, which now has drastically changed the economy of the world.

Chapter 18: World of Computers

As we know today, computers have a colossal effect on the economy. We come across computers or gadgets that use this technology in our own homes, cars, planes, factories, offices, and a variety of other places. The computer has both positive and negative effects on the economy.

On the negative side, it allows automation of manufacturing plants or makes robots that automate machinery and eliminate the need for human intervention. This makes humans redundant in manufacturing to a varying degree currently, leading to a reduction in the opportunities for the average masses to make money to purchase their daily needs for their existence.

On the positive side, it has created a new industry used extensively by people for their daily needs. This has created new professions, such as programmers, web designers, and computer technicians, to name a few. Then, of course, the new industry of computer manufacturing is spread all over the world. Due to its profound effect on the economy, we would add this separate paragraph to understand the computer a little bit more in detail.

ABACUS

Now, let us try to understand how this computer works in the most basic way. The earliest known similar device was called ABACUS. This helped in addition, subtraction, etc., for merchant's long time ago. This apparatus had pebbles or beads strung on a wire in different rows. These pebbles have weights of 1, 10, 100, etc. By moving those to a side of the string, the person could count. For example, a large number of oranges can be counted with this device without having to memorize huge numbers. When the counting is finished, he just adds what is on one side of the device, stored in 10's or 100's as desired. This easily enabled him to know how many oranges he counted without having to keep in mind a large number accurately. In addition, he could do subtraction, multiplication, etc., in a similar way with this gadget.

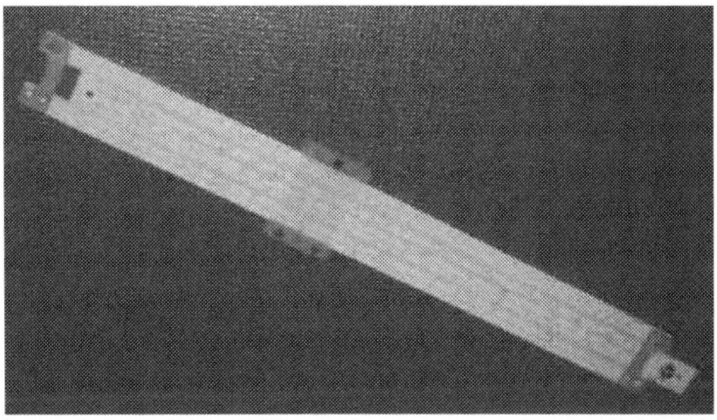

SLIDE RULER

Then came the analog computers. We will not talk about this now as it never caught up as a commonly used device but was used for specific scientific applications only. A good example of such would be the slide rule engineers used for calculations a long time ago when the calculator was not in existence.

COMPUTERS

Today, we have the digital computer, which works on electronic pulses interpreted in binary numbers, such as 1, 2, 4, 8, 16, which are powers of base 2. Surprisingly, the only function computers do is addition only. Every other function is derived from addition. For example, to multiply 5 by 10, the computer would add 5 ten times. Similarly, if we want to store the letter 'a' in the computer, it will translate this to a number format and store it. When you want to retrieve it, the computer will reconvert the number back to figure 'a' and display it on the screen. However, I will not go too deep into this but try to give a basic idea as to how a digital computer works due to the influence it now has on our life.

The current computer is an electronic device that executes a predefined action. It takes a command from the user via a keyboard or what is called a program and displays a computed output on a screen or sends the command to another machine in the field or plant. These signals would generally be in the form of electrical signals or such converted to pneumatic or hydraulic power.

To this end, now we will see how a computer substitutes a person or persons to maintain a level of a tank in a process plant. The computer has instructions known as a program. Now, this program tells it to acquire the level of the tank information every millisecond from a signal hardwired to it and display it on a screen called the user interface. In addition, the computer also uses this signal to check against a limit value it gets from the user interface as entered by the operator before to know what height the level of the tank should be maintained at. Now, if the tank level nears the high-level value set by the operator, the computer would send a signal as per the program to a valve fixed to the tank to close it, which is there to fill the tank. This prevents overflow of the tank.

When the level of the tank goes down to a fixed level or below, as set by the operator, it would command this valve to open to fill the tank. This signal controls the valve by energizing an electrical coil from the power derived from the computer signal or an outside power source via a hardware device, such as a relay or similar element. In this manner, the computer, with the help of the program, will maintain the level of the tank without the need for a human opening and closing the valve when the liquid in the tank gets used.

Now, how does the computer handle this information from what we call the program? The computer has a **ROM (Read-Only Memory)**. This memory is pre-coded with a set of instructions on extremely small electronic switches with its status ON or OFF corresponding to a logical state of 1 or 0. A string of these 1 or 0 makes an instruction or command to the computer as to what action it should do next. And such instructions may be coded with 4, 8, 16, 32, or even 64 switch status, 1 or 0 configurations. Then a computer may have thousands to millions of these instructions in a program. Furthermore, this program is permanent, meaning their 1 or 0 status does not disappear on a power loss. This program is called the BIOS or Basic Input-Output System.

Now, we need to understand what is called a clock in a computer. This is in every computer and brings it to life or power it up. These computers can be categorized as embedded, micro, laptop, desktop, and mainframe, depending on how it is used. And they all have certain components—a mechanism to input information, such as a touchscreen monitor, keyboard, etc., the means of output, such as a screen or direct signals to the field, and a CPU or Central Processing Unit where all the calculations take place. This may consist of what we call ROM and a RAM or read-write memory with or without what is called a clock.

The embedded means a small computer embedded in another device, such as a washing machine, to control its speed, cycles, etc. Micro means a dedicated small computer that may handle a specific task in an industrial environment, such as the controls of a dough-mixing machine laid outside of the mixer. The laptop and desktop are the ones we regularly use. The mainframe is a large computer system with many processors, meaning the CPUs, which handle billions of transactions or instructions per second.

The clock mentioned above generates an electrical pulse signal when power is applied to the computer. This is considered the heartbeat of the system. These signals make the computer load information stored in the switches (ROM) to what is known as **RAM (Random-Access Memory)**. This is where the program or instructions are stored, instructing of what we want the computer to do, like to add numbers.

The relationship between the ROM and the RAM is such that the ROM stores what the computer should do on power-up, and the RAM should do as per the computer program. The ROM instructions cannot be changed, but the RAM stores the user program loaded to same via user screen, disk, pen/thumb drive, etc. The user program will be as per the need of the user and may be written in languages, such as Basic, Assembler, Fortran, C, C++,

Python, or many others. These languages are sometimes designed specifically for building certain applications, such as Accounting, Business, and Engineering, etc.

However, these programming languages are in a text format the computer cannot understand but only the programmer. To this end, the computer uses what is known as a compiler or interpreter, which translates this program in the text to strings of 1's and 0's. So, what is in the RAM now as the program is strings of instructions in 1's and 0's.

Now, as mentioned earlier, on power-up and as per the clock pulse, generally, the information in the ROM or BIOS gets loaded to a specific section of the reserved memory area in the RAM. On consequent clock pulses, it makes the computer go through each instruction set in the ROM along with the instructions set in the RAM as per the program. For example, if the operator types something on the computer, the BIOS detects that new information has been entered in the user screen and tells the user program that an entry has been made or input has been done. Now, the user program picks up that entry, and at a certain point of the program, it executes instructions one step at a time to do what it has been instructed to do when such an entry was made by the user.

Due to the rapid advancement of electronics, computers have become much cheaper to make and exceedingly small, which consumes less power. Hence, being made available for wide usage in our economy.

For industrial automation, these computers have taken a specific form called PLCs (Programmable Logic Controllers) or DCS (Distributed Controllers). Notwithstanding the above features in today's world, these computers (PLC or DCS) have been made to communicate or share data between them, increasing the application for industrial automation. This paves the way for automation, in general, making it much more widely applicable or usable. Therefore, what are the features that make computers so special in industrial applications, which we are concerned so much about? They make vast amounts of people unemployed, especially at manufacturing plants, devastating their avenue for economic livelihood.

a) It would execute the same action repeatedly if the user program instructs it to. This translates, for example, to a car assembly plant. A robot with an inbuilt computer would screw bolts in the same location repeatedly as each car passes. Alternatively, weld the same seam repeatedly at the same location in the same way as each car passes by in the assembly line.

b) It would be precise in its operation, which translates to minimal or no errors in the above-said assembly line, unlike humans doing the same work manually. This makes the quality of the work consistent, whether good or bad. In addition, if bad, this could easily be fixed by correcting the program.

c) As said earlier, if the screw position needs to be changed or the weld pattern needs changing, it would need a simple change to the program by the touch of a button in the human interface or the computer screen if the new required pattern is already coded to the existing program, such as a recipe program would be. This eludes the need to retrain humans for the new change. This leads to less downtime and, therefore, higher efficiency and more profits.

d) A machine or a robot driven by a computer will not get tired as humans would. Also, they won't get sick as humans do but keep going as long as there is no mechanical breakdown or unless they run out of bolts or welding rods.

In this context, it is also important to know a couple of more things in relation to computer technology. Firstly, heat is generated inside a computer when electricity or a battery is connected. This limits the computer's performance or stability. Powerful computers have a higher memory capacity along with high speeds of operations. More memory capacity means it utilizes more electronic media as transistors, etc. If more transistors are added, it would need more electricity to operate, which causes heating and subsequent breakdown of the computer.

Scientists or technologists have always tried to add more transistors in different methods and at the same time minimize the heat generated so that computers get more powerful as well as small. This has taken the scientists to a physical limit by making these transistors in near-atomic level from molecule level to create large memory capacities which use less electricity at this level to function. For example, talking about the switches mentioned above, maybe it took several thousand molecules of chemical elements to make one switch. Now at the said atomic level, it may be only a few hundred or less.

That being said, today, computers have a certain drawback when needed to run large complex applications, say in the weather forecast, molecular biology, or in the military, to analyze the trajectory of new hypersonic missiles, where only seconds are left to this end. This is because its operation is sequential. Meaning, it does things step-by-step to analyze information or data stored in the switches as 1's and 0's only. Hence, certain applications would take days to process, even with the fastest computers currently available.

However, now we have started talking about QUBID bits, which means a few hundred atoms would not be used to make the switch, but a subatomic particle of an atom itself, known as the electron, would be used to function as a switch. This is by controlling the spin of the electron to store a logical state of 1 or 0 or anything in between. To this end, even the spin of a photon, from which light is made, would be controlled.

As said before, with single transistors made of many atoms to store 1 or 0, now we can use part of the spin of a single atom to store 0 or 1. Furthermore, as per the direction of the spin of this subatomic particle, we can assign values like 1, 2, 4, 8, etc. Hypothetically speaking, the left spin of an electron would represent 1, right spin 0, topspin 4, and bottom spin 8, whereas earlier, it required many thousands of atoms to this end. However, how this is being done by scientists, we shall not go into detail here as it is not the focus of this book. But giving the reader an idea of future implications of such developments in computer technology may bear down on the current economy because, in our belief system, humans are manipulating the creations of the creator itself for a better or worse.

Now another use of QBITS' ability to store information as logical 1 or 0 or anything in between is that it facilitates the computer program to analyze vast quantities of data in one single step. This translates to, say, one day of work by a mainframe reduced to a few seconds by this type of computer now called Quantum Computers. Now how is that possible? Without going into details, suffice to say, it is possible because all the data to be analyzed can be stored in one string of the electrons or photons used. Earlier, each data condition had to be in one string of switches, and hence the computer had to run through maybe millions of such data strings to come up with the required solution, which now is one string only.

With all these increases in computer power for data processing, we are now talking of Artificial Intelligence or AI. Also, the packing of data has become so dense that we can now have the information in a library stored in a small computer chip.

However, the author thinks that computers will never have this intelligence as they only can do what the program tells them to do. Therefore, if it is AI, it would have to decide on an unexpected situation correctly and accurately all the time for us to rely on it. Some may argue that due to the vast amounts of information we can now store in computers, we could have programs running on probabilities and statistics to accurately predict any outcome that needs to be correctly predicted. If you ask me, I will say who knows? Do you want to take that chance on a medical diagnostic? Maybe it would help to validate a human judgment not to make it.

However, the question arises if all these developments are now contributing to taking society one notch higher in this economy and creating more jobs than they are replacing? To answer this question, we will now look a little more deeply into what is known as industrial automation and see the profound effects computers have in some industries.

Chapter 19: Automation

Automation is when machines make products without human intervention. It uses industrial-type computers called PLC (Programmable Logic Controller) or DCS (Distributed Control System). This is like the computers we have at home, but which can receive information from signals wired or radioed in from the field. They have physical connections called signals wired to the machines in the field, and they sometimes number in tens of thousands. These signals monitor conditions of the process in the field as temperature, flow rates, pressures, etc., and signals going to the field to stop-start motors, open flow valves, etc., as required.

As an example, let us think of a cookie-making plant. In the manual or non-automated mode, a person would be filling a vessel with flour and other ingredients after weighing them and start the motor to manually mixing it. This dough will now manually be placed in a pan and in an oven to bake. In addition, the person would set the temperature and set the time and, when the time expires, would most probably check the color of the cookies and then take them out when he thinks they are fully cooked or baked.

After baking, he would take the cookies out and let them cool, and then put them into small containers and box them for shipping out to the customers. If this process is manual, as stated, it will take several people to do all this work. Moreover, due to human temperament, the quality of the cookies may not be consistent, as errors may occur when measuring the ingredients for the cookie mix or determining if the cookies are baked. Furthermore, there would be medical issues associated with some workers who would be doing the same type of action all the time, known as Carpel Tunnel syndrome. Some may even be burned by hot ovens. Additionally, some of the employees may get sick, and the owner would have to make alternate plans to ensure his cookies are still baked. As a business person, no one would want to lose the customers to another baker. Now, we will compare this process to the said automation process.

In the automation process, the ingredients for making the cookies, such as flour or sugar, will initially be put into silos or large containers with an outlet at the bottom linked to a conveyor belt. From this point, what comes out at the end of the process would be cookies already made to a predefined quality and recipe. This means the ingredients to make the cookies would come out of the silos via a conveyor belt. This is weighed to proportion via scales and mixed in a mixer to the right consistency, which is automatically monitored and then get poured into the cooking molds. It is then sent to a baking machine on a conveyer belt and baked to a set time and consistency. The water content and the color will be automatically monitored to this end. Now, let's take this a little further. The baked cookies would also be automatically packed into different containers and then boxed and made ready to be shipped as per the orders. All this will be controlled by this industrial computer.

Now, let's suppose the manufacturer wants to make different types of cookies as per customer requirements. For this, it would only require the operator to select another predefined recipe. If necessary, even make a new recipe as a program, download it to the computer, and run it to make the new cookies. The machine will make the new cookie if it has the basic mechanical items already in place, such as the silos and conveyor system. What this means is that if the new product requires a lesser number or the same number of silos for the raw material storage, then the owner could make any new type of cookie very easily. Meaning, it would only take one person at the computer and few seconds to load the new program into the computer or the PLC. These programs are called recipe programs and only need to be selected from the screen if it is already in the computer.

Now, let me give an example of what may happen soon that can put many farmworkers out of employment. Let us consider an orange plantation that gets a new machine, which would have several mechanical arms. In each arm, there would be a gripping mechanism and a detector to smell ripe fruits and a camera. When the camera detects an orange in the tree, it would automatically guide the arm to it. Then if the smell says it is ready, the machine commands the gripping mechanism to pluck it. The gripping mechanism would be able to detect the slipping of orange once it gets a hold of it. Also, it won't apply too much gripping power on the orange and damage it.

The machine would then move between the orange groves as per a GPS signal through a computer, which would keep it moving in a predefined path between the orange groves. Let us consider that there are several arms doing the plucking of selected oranges. Here, the computer, of course, ensures that the arms do not collide and try to pluck the same orange by keeping track of the positions of the arms. When the bucket is full, it will automatically go to the processing center for unloading. All the pickers and associated drivers' jobs are now lost while gaining a few for maintaining these machines. A question to ponder over now would be to gauge the number of people required to produce these machines. For this study, we say 50, which would be conservative, and another 100 for its parts supply chain.

To understand this, for a 1000-acre orange farm, say the farmer employees 20 people to pluck the fruits, do the weeding, etc. We need to remember there are automated machines for weeding too. But there would be hundreds of such orange farms. However, if

100 such farms now lost 2000 jobs, with about 150 jobs added for manufacturing these machines, not only for orange plucking but even many other fruits using the same principle by making a few changes to the program, we can understand the implications.

In a future world, it is possible that everything would be automated. This means millions of people would lose their jobs. Nevertheless, there is an argument that new jobs would be created for making the machines and maintaining them. However, these would be minuscule compared to the jobs that would be lost in the industry if they were manual, as discussed above in the orange farm example. With the need to make products cheaper to compete in the marketplace, the effect of Industrial Automation would be profound on job losses for the average masses, causing large adverse effects in the economy. This would restrict the flow of wealth to a few among the masses, leading even to mass unrest in time.

Chapter 20: World of Robotics

It would be interesting to formulate an idea as to how the world economy would be when robots are doing most of the work. There may be few exceptions to this, such as household work, painting, specifically gourmet cooking, decorating, medical doctors, nurses, building construction workers and robotic programmers, etc. Also, there would be some research scientists, such as physicists still doing research on future robotic developments, chemists, pharmacists, ambulance workers, farmers, soldiers, and others doing similar work. Now we will briefly see how this employment would pan out in the robotic world.

Doctors – A gadget used at home will diagnose the medical issues and send a report to the database and a robotic doctor. The robotic doctor would then prescribe the medication, and this information would be sent to a human doctor for final approval. Once this happens, the prescription would be sent to a pharmacy, which would then automatically fill the prescription and would automatically post it to the patient or even call the patient to pick it up at a certain location if it is urgent. And if the matter is urgent, the robotic doctor would advise the patient to come to the human doctor for further diagnosis. A remote pharmacist will still oversee this filling. This all would cause at least a 50% reduction of family doctors and pharmacists required. If the patient is still sick, they would now demand to see a specialist doctor who would get the report as before and see the patient. So, some demand for specialist doctors would still exist, or AI would now help with this.

Nurses – Patients go to the hospital by self-driven cars. The car stops at the emergency room entrance. A human by the door helps the patient to a self-driving trolley and makes an in-situ computer medical diagnosis. As per the diagnosis, the trolley goes to different rooms with an attendant, who would prepare the patient as necessary. The robotic trolley then takes the patients to different rooms for surgery, x-ray, MRI, etc., as per the computer, depending on the diagnosis. Subsequently, the patient is then taken by trolley to the relevant ward. At this point, the nurse would take over, and the patient would be placed on a bed. At the same time, the doctor related would automatically be summoned to the hospital through a computer system via a Wi-Fi link to his beeper may be as now. Once the doctor attends to the patient and confirms the diagnosis made by the robot, a prescription would be sent to the pharmacy via his smart computer. The pharmacy would dispatch the medication to the ward nurse in charge for its administration via a robotic carrier. In addition, at the same time, the robotic doctor attached to the patient's bed would keep a 24/7 monitoring of the patient, negating the requirements of nurses or house doctors to visit the patient most of the time.

Farmer - Concerning farmers and robots would be doing most of the farming. The machines would plow the field, check the soil, add fertilizer if necessary, plant the trees, pluck the harvest, and bring the same to the processing location. All this by using GPS signals to know its location as per the computer program defining what exactly it should do, translating it to mechanical actions via actuators and sensors. The farmer would only decide when to do what and start the machine with the necessary program initiated.

Military – Interesting to see the effect of this on the military, which now employs thousands of soldiers and support staff. Ships and planes would now be autonomous. For example, on detecting an incoming unauthorized aircraft, an alarm would be activated at a 24/7 monitoring station. If detected as an enemy aircraft or vessel, a preprogrammed missile or such would take off by itself and try to intercept the intruder. On the other hand, if there is a war far away, robots would be deployed via large transport aircraft, which themselves would be automated, and the robotic soldiers would be dropped off to fight the enemy. No airfields would be required as these robots would jump out of the aircraft in parachutes or when the robotic aircraft hovers very low to the ground. Now, the armed robots would shoot at anything that has metal in their hand or does not carry a device emitting a friendly signal and will take over an area as required. Human troops will subsequently visit the location and will take over control. Now soldiers will only be required to maintain things, such as planes, ships, etc. Even in this case, robots can be used for refueling and other tasks as appropriate.

Therefore, in the end, what jobs would be left for the masses? There would, of course, be some human employment like controlling and the manufacturing of robots. The government comprising a few individuals would be making decisions as to the future directions of the country, such as decisions on war, etc. As mentioned before, doctors, nurses, farmers, police, military, judiciary, and the leisure industry cannot be completely automated. It is my guess that all these would be less than 10% of the population, and less than a few hundred would be the government.

In all, there would hardly be any employment opportunities for the masses. Of course, now people would start rioting against the government. The question is, what can the government do to this end? First, there is the question of food. For this, the government would be giving all the population a monthly stipend to buy their basic needs, such as food and clothing.

Secondly, the government would have to provide the people prefabricated housing modules made by robots for their housing or hire some groups of people to put up their houses. The medical and education will be free for all. So, now the issue of food, medicine, and housing is satisfied. Then there, of course, would be some extra money from the government to go on occasional vacations. There would hardly be the need for any savings by this 90% of the unemployed as they now have a guaranteed income from the government and even some money for travel etc. Most importantly, all the money the government gives will flow back to the government as taxes or direct payments for purchases from the government entities. The few members of the government would have an egoistic satisfaction, knowing they are the most elite and powerful, and all their needs too would be fulfilled as they desire.

Then, within this 90%, there would be some who may earn extra money to spend by working and running leisure industry in the form of hotels, tourism, etc., where the effect of robots would be less felt. However, the government would tax them greatly, even up to 70 -80% of their net profit or wages, to recover what they give the 90% to spend. By the way, people other than those who are in this type of business as sanctioned by the government would be prohibited from savings to ensure the money flows back to the government and is not stuck somewhere in a safe. Even the money saved will not have any interest paid on it.

To keep that 90% happy, the government would fill any upcoming vacancies of the government due to various reasons by having raffle draws among the 90% to select qualified personnel, which may include entrepreneurs and scientists. The government would fund their projects for a limited time as current corporations do. If they do not perform, they will be fired.

Now, it would be the job of entrepreneurs and scientists to take the economy up one notch at a time. If they achieve success, they will be granted recognition among the masses, and all their economic desires will be met, including that of their immediate family members.

The government would now claim that this is a people's government and be hopeful that there would be no riots or uprisings by the masses against the ruling hierarchy or government or bureaucracy as it is a people's government. Then they would have the right to punish anyone who goes against them as they would justify this as they are the representative of the people by the people.

Then, as for law and order, there will mostly be robots under human control. For example, if there is a murder, a central monitoring station would analyze what has happened and identify the culprits. There would be cameras in almost all the places, even in people's houses. Of course, the recordings in the houses would only be analyzed with an order of a judge for privacy concerns. A robot would now be sent to apprehend and bring the culprit to a detention center. A human judge would now look at the evidence, and robots will execute the punishment by sending that person to a jail run by robots.

As for wars, they would be fought by robots under the direction of a human from decentralized locations, making it difficult for the other country to annihilate them totally in a single strike.

Chapter 21: Value of Money

Everyone wants money in this life. The more you have, the more one wants. As per the previous discussions, we have also seen the importance of money in a society to safeguard the economic wellbeing of the masses. This is to ensure wealth distribution to the masses through job opportunities to make a living.

Now, we will take the example of a poor person starving with no money and then getting some. The initial money he or she gets would be of immense value to that person so he or she could buy food to eat to satisfy hunger. More money too would be of use as that person may buy a house for shelter, clean clothing for health, etc. So, after all these initial needs are met, that person will go on to buy maybe a private plane and then put enough money in the bank for the same purpose to last his or her lifetime. Then some more for his or her family and more for generations to come. However, as that person's needs get satisfied, what that person could do with the money get diminishes other than to say to the society how rich that person is, meaning satisfying a false ego.

However, some would rightly see the value of money to be enhanced by giving to charity as self-satisfying without any limit to such satisfaction. For example, funding cancer research, building hospitals for the poor, feeding the poor, building shelters for the homeless, providing education for the poor, providing housing for the disabled soldiers, building shelters for animals, etc. from which they derive contentment or self-satisfaction much more than in building factories, starting a new business, traveling all over the world and staying in the best hotels or anything else that person could think of for self-indulgence.

I think by giving to charity, one is never fed up with seeing the results of such activities as long as one lives or maybe even in the next life. Spending money, buying luxury vehicles, luxury houses, private planes, etc., inflates one's ego only momentarily. They would soon get fed up with them and will want to upgrade them further, and so on with no end in sight. However, one may argue that these purchases contribute to the economy. In fact, spending for such luxuries is better than keeping it in a bank account as a saving unless giving for charity or the betterment of the human and even animals.

For example, we will consider a billionaire buying an extra comfortable chair in order to relax. Soon, he will be fed up with it and find interest elsewhere or will now want a better chair than this, and so on without an end. Consider the same rich person building an ultra-modern cancer hospital that offers free treatment. Now, if that person starts to look at all the children coming out of the hospital fully cured with smiles on their faces with their caregivers, would that person ever get fed up with seeing this? So, what would be the value of his money to him or her at this time?

Chapter 22: Religion or Beliefs

Religion helps one overcome fear, pain and suffering through the strength of their beliefs. It even allows overcoming the bad economic climate in this life with the belief that in the next life, God would provide a great economic opportunity where all the needs will be satisfied. So now, GOD has come to the economy.

Hence, the first question which comes to one's mind is, what is that people believe, and what does this have to do with the economy for people in this life? As for the afterlife, in the simplest sense, it is the belief in a higher being known as God through which one anticipates going to a place with better economic opportunity, good health, plenty of money to spend as desired, and where all the wishes come true. Maybe even to have more money, despite already having sufficient for a comfortable life.

However, as we will discuss later, the economy is one's satisfaction with the mind. For example, if a person is poor, money-wise, and hardly has enough to eat but is very satisfied with what he has, then the economy of that individual can be considered near 100%. The same applies in the opposite manner, where a person having all the comforts and is still unhappy, then the economy of that person could be considered near 0%.

If humans had everything they desired freely available to them and they did not grow old and die, there would be no need for religion or faith in God. However, due to the shortage of basic needs in our lives, sometimes leading to hunger or sickness, we ask for help from this highest authority from time to time. To me, this is the same as going to a doctor when sick, going to a mafia don when we need something which may be illegal, or in verse even to a politician. Basically, when everything fails, we then plead to this entity we call God the creator or sub-God (not the creator but any other being we believe has that power) to grant us our wishes or ease our suffering in this life. For this, we offer our allegiance to this entity or even make sacrifices of live animals by cutting their heads off in a brutal fashion. This is mostly when the creator God could easily kill anything he wants, including newborn babies or babies to be born. In the worst case in history, people have even made human sacrifices to please the God they believed in, to this end. For example, in some countries in the old days, the ignorant high priest made a human sacrifice of young maidens by stabbing them in the heart or cutting their heads off when there was no rain or the harvest was poor.

From time to time, we have heard the name God and references have been made to a creator of this universe or of Earth. Humans, for a very long time, have attributed everything unknown or uncontrollable by them to the work of this God or related entities we call sub-Gods here. This would include the sun god, god of rain, god of punishment, or even god of education.

However, in this discussion, our reference would be to God the creator. Others must be one level lower than the creator God as they only exist because the creator God made the suns, moons, and the universe as we know of. Unfortunately, even worthless rocks are speeding around our solar systems. Hence, the most important to us will be the creator God, who invariably must have the final word on any godly matter, including our earthly existence. Now, we must consider whether the creator of this universe is only a single God. Alternatively, is it multiple Gods? This we do not know. However, for this situation, we consider there is only one God in existence.

For centuries, people brutally killed each other in thousands to appease this Creator or God. As an example, certain religious crusades from Europe went to the Middle East mainly to liberate the birthplace of the son of God from another set of believers, who had a different name for the same God, killing each other in thousands. Both believe that there is only one such God that exists. This was probably to appease their God, as, after all, the believers of this God from Europe did not want to leave the place of birth of the son of God in the hands of the believers of the same God but of a different name. Then there are other believers who have another name for the same God and slaughter countless millions of animals to offer their blood to this entity, saying it is their God, especially in Asia.

I have even seen these people throw live chickens to the fire to this end. Nevertheless, the irony of this situation is, had they been born to a family of another belief, they would be killing the other believers to appease the same God.

Then, of course, there are a few who, for some reason or other, change their original belief by conviction and kill others, even though they may believe in the same God, but maybe the messenger was different. Dwelling little more on this, it may not necessarily be because of a conviction but may be due to financial inducement, a better position in society, or a sincere belief in experiencing a miracle. It can also be due to death threats to oneself or even family members by the believers of another God who has a different name, as said before, for the same God. So, the bottom line is, you could kill another human being if their belief has a different name for the same God or the messenger from the same God was different. It was said when some Europeans conquered other parts of the world a long time ago, they went with their holy book in one hand, a sword in the other, and the conquered inhabitants had to choose between the two.

As for killing non-believers, some think such actions would grant them better economic status in this life or at the least next life as his God would be pleased with the devotion shown to him even though the current societies consider such actions to be barbaric with a penalty of death for such deeds. In any event, we do not know of any person now or in the past receiving such economic benefits for these murderous acts. For example, we do not know of any such ruler suddenly being benefited with gold, gems, etc., for such deeds in the past. Otherwise, all these murderers would be super rich with no disease or sickness. But they probably end up suffering in jail with a death sentence in most of the countries.

Even with these violent acts to appease their God in the past, they would suffer when their child, mother, father, or wife/husband died. Alternatively, the saying goes, it is the 'will of God,' and your suffering does not matter in this life as in the next life all will be good, and your economy would be 100% then. Hence, forget about the suffering in this life.

As for the Creator, common sense says there cannot be more than a single creator if there is any. There may be the possibility of a family of gods with one creating Earth and one Saturn and another the moon etc. Then, of course, the one who created Earth may be the most successful one as the other planets are dead. Meaning, Earth is the only habitable one we know of, and the rest of the planets are uninhabitable to humans as far as we know. That is, the ones we know of lack water and oxygen or have burning or freezing temperatures, making it inhabitable for humans, God's subjects.

However, let us look at the God who made Earth and see whether He did a humane job, which means whether He was compassionate to his creations, the man and the woman, or at the least to the animals. Maybe all this sickness humans suffer now, which is a book full, is humane according to His vision and not ours. Maybe, all the creations were trial and error ones, and Earth is the one He had the most success in. The question arises, is He the supreme creator, or were there additional ones with more power and vision than this one as there is supposed to be wonderful heaven as well as terrible hell before Earth was created? Or maybe the hell came later to put the unbelievers there.

If we believe in our senses, we know humans have evolved over time from cave dwellings to present high-rise dwellers. In this sense, it is rational to expect that He made us ape-like hairy beasts in the beginning. Then, of course, He had to decide how He was going to increase our numbers. Well, it could have been that we just popped up in different shapes and sizes from time to time as He wished. Also, He could have done it like an amoeba, just splitting when He required us to do so or growing new ones from our bodies and falling off like nuts or suddenly appear automatically fabricated from the resources of Earth, such as air, heat, etc.

He must have then thought of a greater idea, the 'Women.' Then you wonder how He contemplated women to be. Are there women in His kingdom? Otherwise, how did this great mind give the reproductive organs and then build a desire in humans for the propagation to take place? To me, even to contemplate such a thing tells a lot about His thinking. It's difficult for my minuscule brain to understand such a mind. Then, this entity is not a man but the supreme Creator. So, who am I to understand His thinking but just obey as some wants.

Now, after going to all the trouble of making worthless planets, super-hot sun, etc., He had the compassion of cooling down Earth and making it habitable for His creation. Did He think of the fact that His creation would not be able to withstand His initially created Earth with boiling lava etc.? Was He obligated to another power as who created heat? Did His initial creation had to wait till the heat cooled down, or did it withstand all this but then automatically adjusted itself to meet the new environment, as Darwin said?

If this is the case, Darwin must have had the intellect to be the closest to the Creator than all of us. In some books, it was stated that Earth was made in one day, and then the sun was made, and then, in the end, the man and the woman were made. If this was the case, the oxygen in the air too had to come into existence before the man and the woman in order to breathe, or maybe they did not initially breathe, and only after eating the forbidden apple did they feel the need to do so. However, now we find that life form also exists deep in the sea under tons of water pressure and in pitch darkness even without oxygen where humans would be crushed to a pulp. Wonder when this situation was created and why.

Now, consequent to creating these human entities classified into two genders, man and woman, was He again obligated to other powers, such as time and decay, and the need to ensure conception takes place and to have fresh female embryos to this end? Oops! He must have been mad at the woman and cursed this species with monthly pain and suffering. Maybe this is because she had enticed the male to eat the apple.

On the other hand, religions mainly guide their followers to become good citizens of society. Most well-known religions ask their followers to give some of their wealth to charity in order to cleanse themselves of desire. To keep the floor clean where one lives etc., for a hygienic life. The giving in my thinking is also to show kindness to the needy or the sick when they are hit by unsatisfactory economic conditions. By the way, being the ultimate designer, making all these planets, suns, and moons, did He made a mishap by creating a species in-between of the man and the woman. On the other hand, did some other heavenly joker who had put the screws in the Creator's creations cause this? Who knows?

Now, notwithstanding all this, He must have thought how to punish more of his creation for eating an apple. Well, consider poor pigs eating human excrete in some countries. Obviously, it seems nice and of a pleasant smell to this animal. Then the man and the woman he created make this excrete, which is full of stink to us. Not only this, He made them carry it inside of them until it is eliminated for the poor pigs to eat.

Now, wait a minute! That is not going to be good enough. What about making them the man and the woman now we call humans to excrete smelly liquids from every hole in their body?

Even though that is not enough, they were given what is called diseases. Let the skin, guts, or every part of the body rot and then cripple and then kill it. Hang on, still not happy? Why not kill their young ones early and make them suffer or maybe sometimes kill them in thousands through a tsunami, earthquake, etc., or even send some heavenly rocks to hit Earth and destroy every living thing in it – man, woman, child, baby, animals – with all his believers too? It must have been some fun to even make some near misses so they will shiver in fear. However, there are followers who pray to this supposed to be God and ask for salvation from bad economic conditions they sometimes face in this world.

Moreover, is the creator of this world the one whom we call God, or is it the devil that created Earth, the man, and the woman? God must be an entity that is kind, compassionate, understanding, etc., as per what we believe in. However, I am thankful for one thing. He did not change the position of the mouth and the anus. That would have been some punishment. On the other hand, He did not also make our skin transparent. Just imagine that scenario. So, we need to be thankful for this.

The talk of the town is that all this punishment is because someone ate an apple, as said earlier. For that, He made His creation suffer in billions. Not even the newly born or to-be-born to His most adherent faithful disciples are spared whichever way they believe in him. They were all subjected to the same suffering and decay and death, the same as the non-believers. So as far as it seems, there is no benefit in this life being His believers.

Well, He must have still not been content. What about the food He created for His creation called the animals? Should I do the same to them what I did to the humans even if they did not eat an apple? Well, He must have thought that this would not matter and did the same thing to them or even worse. After all, nothing can happen without His knowledge. Now, 'let me see what I can do worse.' 'Why not let them eat each other ALIVE?' Not only are they eaten alive, but they would go to a place called stomach alive when swallowed whole, which is pitch dark and full of acid to be burnt little at a time and die slowly. One can only visualize such pain they would suffer before death.

Consider the situation of a deer chased by a lion, wolf, or other predator running for its dear life as fast as it can. In the end, it gets exhausted and just stops for the predator to eat it alive piece by piece until it dies. Similarly, for example, when an eagle catches a baby rabbit, it eats it piece by piece alive by pecking the flesh each time in small bits and maybe even the eye at times. Now consider you being the baby rabbit.

With all this and more, this God the creator must have been incredibly happy in His handy work and enjoying it. However, with mercy, God has put us at the top of the food chain, where humans eat everything uncaringly, including putting live lobsters in hot water to kill it, so its flesh tastes better, and even throw live shrimps on a hot plate as some people do in some countries. Humans even chop off the fins of sharks and drop them back to the sea to die in pain at the bottom of the ocean just because they do not want to waste time killing it as more fins could be cut during that time. It is even said that in some countries in Asia, the king would eat the brain of the monkey when it was alive to improve his manhood.

We, humans, are called God's children so kind and compassionate, so much so that sometimes we put a baby sheep into a lion's den while it screams in fear and even poops so that the lion could eat the baby sheep alive as a fresh meal. This is to give humans the enjoyment of seeing the lion nice and well-fed. We would not think twice about killing billions of cows, sheep, chickens, etc., to eat, but at the same token, may nurse a sick animal to health.

I have seen in this country a certain animal in a cage being fed by live mice. The animal had already eaten one and was resting on a branch of a tree in the cage. The other mouse was trying to get out of the cage but kept failing. So, it tried to make itself small by curling like a ball in the corner of the cage at the same time pooping in fear. What a sight for the Creator!

What is this hypocrisy? It seems God made us like animals, not a civilized man and a woman initially. That may be the reason why for example, in World War I, during trench warfare, when one side charged over the trenches, they just knifed each other using that animal instinct, when some of them were people whom we previously called teachers or family men. Nowadays, people kill animals and roast them on fires and eat them for fun or eat them half-cooked, calling it medium rare or rare as our ancestors supposed to have done or raw dipped in a sauce. Does this prove our animal history?

However, we cannot blame God because He gave us free will, and we messed it up. Nevertheless, I wonder what a cow, pig, or a chicken had done to make Him so angry with them. They did not have free will. He must have had a special relationship with them. He made them so that the other animals and, of course, humans can eat them in billions every second. I wonder what they did to Him.

On the other hand, did the Creator have a soft spot for the animals too? After all, if humans did not clean after defecation, they would stink as hell in no time. However, animals do not have to clean themselves after defection as their excretions did not have to touch other body areas prior to falling to the ground. And then, the point of excretion gets covered by a tail or some similar apparatus.

So, does it seem that by mistake, the humans have their excretion location exposed to such an outside body area so that excretion could touch the surrounding body? And this compels us to clean ourselves thoroughly around the location to avoid the stink. Some animals and humans also pass smelly gas after eating, a way of the nature of human creation? Or did the devil require it to be so? As that smell was pleasing to him, being the devil.

As said earlier and per our history, He also sometimes sends missiles from outer space to kill us by the drove as asteroids. To Him, it must be like throwing stones at us and seeing how many dies in one go. Additionally, He must have been so cruel to such an unbelievable extent to send His son to this world and have him nailed to a cross with thorns on His head to die in pain. I wonder whether He was laughing when blood oozed out when nails were hammered into His hands and legs or when sharp thorns dug into His head.

By the way, has anyone become better now than before after this bloodletting? It must be for the next generations only or still to be born someday, hopefully? The important thought to ponder over is, is this was done by a good God to appease the devil and ease the suffering of humanity that was put upon the humans by this devil.

Does this good God also want to take us out from this suffering by asking us to do good deeds in life and defeat the devil who created this world? If this is a possibility, the irony of it is, we kill each other to appease this devil with animal slaughter and do not live a life of good conduct in order to get near to the real God if there is one.

Still, we cannot be angry with Him because He sent us a message through someone many years ago to believe in Him.

However, there still are and have always been many millions who do not believe in this God and may deserve this punishment. Then there are many millions who do and pray to Him diligently. But it does not seem to matter to Him as they too get the same punishment. On the other hand, is this because the devil is more powerful than God, and He is powerless, and the sacrifice of His son has had no effect on the devil either?

In addition, one wonders whether the devil or the Creator put the shit system in the humans after they ate the apple or before. Alternatively, maybe the shit system was there in the initial creation but was made to stink when they ate the apple. By the way, as a kind deed, He may have created the pig later, after seeing the shit lying around.

All this is not to insult or bring disrepute to one's beliefs but to put facts as it is and to point out what we are doing to appease something that we need to keep miles away from.

To me, God is a compassionate, understanding, and forgiving entity and not a vindictive, cruel, or ruthless entity. To me, God does exist. In this world, they are our parents, good teachers, or laypeople who preach well even though misguided. Then, I believe in sub-Gods as well as devils by one's own experience. A good example is this location in a country, depicting a form that is supposed to be a sub-God. In addition, whenever I experience great difficulty in my life, and when I make an appeal to this entity, most of the time, the difficult situation eases. Thus far, this entity has never failed me. In return, I try to pass good thoughts to this entity in the hope this entity could benefit from the same.

On the other hand, seeing people who are supposed to be His high priests cheat and abuse fairness in the very same location and knowing that no justice gets done to them, one tends to wonder why the sub-God did not punish these people. Then it strikes me that a real sub-God does not punish people, but it is the devil who does that.

Then there are the near-death experiences by people who claim they have seen the creator God or the son of this God or Angels from heaven. This includes a very close contact of mine. As it goes, during a simple medical procedure, this person was temporally made unconscious. During the same period, apparently, this person felt amazing peace and tranquility and saw what looked like a carriage fully garlanded with flowers just by a river. Someone asked that person to come to the carriage. At the same time, the person heard his name being called by someone to wake up and call the doctor. Now, who later narrated to that person what had happened as this person was apparently as per medical term passing?

In the same token, other believing people would swear that they have had the same experience with whom they call angels, the God itself, or even have experienced hell. A friend of mine was so terrified of going to hell till he came back to this life again in a near-death experience. As far as I know, he changed his life for the better. But the irony of this is, it seems they all see the God they believe in when having this near-death experience.

In my opinion, the name is irrelevant, whether we call them angels or sub-Gods, as they do not have a religion. They are entities in another dimension or realm that want to help humans and then cherish and dwell on their good thoughts for some reason. So, they appear in locations where people gather to do such good deeds on their behalf, irrespective of their denominations.

Similarly, there may be devils who may help the humans in some of these locations to hurt, kill or do bad things to other humans in return for the blood of animals or even sacrifice of humans as done in ancient times. What needs to be kept in mind is that more than the humans associating with sub-Gods, the humans associating with the devils will not have any reprieve if they make them mad and may even pay with their lives.

To this end, I like to narrate my own experience in this regard. I was maybe about 6-7 years old during this incident. My parents believed in witchcraft. So, for every little sickness, my mother used to call on this old lady to see whether anyone had done something bad to my father for him to get sick as he was supposed to have made many enemies due to his political work. In one instance, this old lady was looking at a black spot at the back of a saucer through the light of a land oil lamp. Without going into details, being curious on this day, as I saw she was not on her bench looking at this black spot through this light, I started doing the same.

Somehow now, I was deep into this black spot through this light which I do not know how even to this date. After some time, I saw a figure with a monkey face wearing glittering clothes directing me to a location in our backyard. Instantly, I jumped up and threw all the apparatus and screamed. My mother and this woman then came running to me, and as it happened, I never saw this woman again until I was fully grown up. Also, after many years, I saw the same type of figure drawn on a wall in a religious place. So as for me, I believe in other dimensions where these sub-Gods or devils may be present.

In the same token, I go to this place in this country every other year or so to give food to the poor and other offerings to this sub-god. The main building in this regard is surrounded by sand. On one of these visits, the sand around this location was so hot that no one in my family could walk a small distance to the main building as shoes of any kind were not allowed around this location. I was much distraught about the situation as I had come a long way from overseas to this end and was flying back in the next few hours, and I wanted my grandchildren to go inside this building. Something told me to try again. So, I put my foot on the sand again to walk to this building. This time it was not hot, and I could walk through it. This was within seconds of the previous experience. As we know, sand does not get hot or cold instantly. The point here is there are things in this world we do not understand and only experience either for good or bad.

All the beliefs in the world that we call religion ask us to believe in a God the creator or his messenger, whose handy work we discussed earlier. The only exception to this is Buddhism, to my understanding, where the question of God is not the issue but one's emancipation by one's true understanding of what we call 'self.' This is as to what this 'self' is undergoing in this world. By this true understanding, as per Buddhism, we are supposed to gain the ability to defeat the devils' agonies bestowed on this self or us, never to happen again.

Thus, by the said true understanding, we get the ability to reach an economic status of 100% via mental satisfaction irrespective of what gets thrown at us, such as hunger, sickness, loss of loved ones, etc. Later, we will discuss how Buddha said this could be achieved. For the atheist, nothing matters if life is good, it is good.

If bad, suck it up as there is no one to go for help. Then, of course, they forget an important fact. That if they are born again to this world or go to hell or to another world, what is the situation? Meaning, you may face the same situation or worse in the next life unless you go to heaven, as some say.

In brief, it is interesting to look at how this human being called Siddhartha Gautham or later named **Buddha,** who was born in India about 2600 years ago as a prince in line for the crown, understood the economic, psychological, or mental situation we face in this life.

His consequent teaching after becoming a Buddha or an Enlightened one, as what he understood, seems to be of different focus from all other such teachings of prophets we know of. Apparently, he has done this by looking into the functioning of our own inner mind through deep meditation or as commonly referred to as "how it ticks and why it ticks."

Basically, he had found that this inner mind is the one that gives us desires and attachments to earthly things, leading to self-ego, which causes us all the suffering in this world. And the origin of this attachment and consequent self-ego has been due to inputs received to our mind from our senses, such as the eye, nose, ear, touch, and tongue. Our inner mind would then process these inputs, analyze what they are, give it an identity as per what is already stored in mind or make a new one altogether, and finally cling to it if it provides even temporary economic or physical satisfaction. But Buddha found that by virtue of correctly understanding these inputs as only representing a temporary phenomenon and thereby not clinging to it, our economy can be made 100% or what he called achieving the state of **Arahant** in this life, which is supposed to lead to the state of **Nirvana**.

So, what exactly is Arahant, which is supposed to be the last stage of four stages that can be achieved in this life, leading to Nirvana after death? According to Buddha's teaching, it is all based on what is called 'Dependent Arising' or 'Cause and Effect' theory. All this means is cause gives rise to effect. The effect, in turn, gives rise to cause. The reason for cause mainly is our greed, aversion, and ignorance. So, as I understand, Arahant mainly means a person who has totally eradicated these bad traits never to appear again in their mind and includes many other virtues too. Importantly, these states of the mind are to be achieved in this life and not the next life.

Nirvana is supposed to be an achievement that would stop this birth, rebirth cycle altogether due to the elimination of the said causes for rebirth. Then the question arises as to whether this is the annihilation of oneself. Apparently, this is not the case. To my understanding, this is like the extinguishing of a flaming candle.

The flame is due to ingredients in the wax that cause it to ignite and light up due to heat. The wax is made by humans to form the candle. In our life, heat is the greed that ignites the candle and consequent karma that sustains the hot or painful candlelight.

Translated to living beings, wax is the embryo created at conception. So, if the greed leading to karma is not there, the embryo would not have a life or ignition, hence no flame as in the candle and no pain of heat. In this situation, greed has caused karma in another life. Which now makes life in this new embryo. So had there been no greed in the past life, this embryo would not have a life and just be part of the universe in peace forever, without burning or suffering as we do now. Though sometimes, momentarily, we think everything is great until it hits you without fail as death or sickness, just to mention a few as before.

He also said that he is not the only Buddha but one of several that will appear or has appeared before in this universe time to time in the intervals of 'eons.' Most importantly, to me, he apparently valued his disciples who learn and practice what he taught, even if they live far away and do not even see him, unlike the ones who may be following him, for his good grace and do not practice his teachings. That said, according to him, he too has a teacher. This was the 'Dhamma' that he had mastered or the way of the universe.

All this shows Buddha's humility. Being born a prince with all the comforts, he left all that for a monastic life to find a way out of this samsara or the birth cycle that we know causes endless pain and suffering. He then went to the most well know and knowledgeable teachers at that time without success to find the answer he sought by practicing their way of meditation. Then, after a period, he punished his body by starvation, thinking this was the way to do it without success. This was due to a belief at that time that the end of suffering can be achieved by taming the mind by punishing the body and with this could reach higher states of existence where there is no pain but all the good things only after death.

For me, the point here is the importance of the mind. Through deep meditation on his own, he realized this is not the case, and the path was neither extreme of overindulgence of pleasures to the body nor by punishing the body. This was called the middle path, and he initially disclosed this to his friends of long ago who were only there when he was torturing his body to this end and left him subsequently in the first sermon called Dhammacakkappavattana Sutra' or disclosure. It sheds light on the eight-fold practices that a person can do to achieve this state of Arahant, which we mentioned before.

This was based on four fundamental truths as he saw. The first was 'Dukka,' meaning life is unsatisfactory. The second was 'the cause for Dukka,' meaning what is the reason for this un-satisfactoriness, which he mentioned was primarily greed and then delusion, etc. The third was 'is there a way out of this Dukka?' This, he basically stated, was the elimination of such traits, as mentioned before. The fourth was 'what is the path to the cessation of this Dukka?' This, he stated, was the eight-fold path.

As the background to this disclosure is deep, one can read it up and make up their own minds, maybe with little practice of this disclosure.

Here, I am not using the word 'teachings' but disclosures because, to me, something becomes teaching only after it has been proven as a fact. If someone says they are teaching something, then it must be a fact or the truth. However, what is disclosed can only be a fact and only after one's own experience practicing it.

Further to the above, his disclosures were so different from other preachers of his time, as the saying goes, 'sky to the earth.' Another thing that intrigued me to study what he has taught was his instructions not to take his disclosures as the truth. But practice what he has said and see the results and then decide for oneself. Secondly, he had never proclaimed that people should worship him or obey him. But had said in a society one has to respect whoever deserves respect. This we know helps society to keep order, hence develop its economy at the same time.

Then some may think these disclosures are all about suffering or very pessimistic teaching as it draws attention to things as death, sickness, sorrow, etc. However, when we study his disclosures more deeply, we find it is just the opposite, which means they are extremely optimistic. I understood this with the help of the following example.

Say someone has fallen in a large hole in the ground and has tried different ways to get to the top without success and is now sick, hungry, etc. In this hole, there are many thorns with flowers, which also bloom with a nice scent and subsequently perish with a bad smell. Now, someone says to this person that there is a way to come out of the hole by following a certain path which he had discovered when he too was in this hole earlier. Also, as long as you are in this hole, enjoy the blooming of flowers but know they will perish and start to smell in time. Hence, do not get attached to those and be aware of the hurtful thorns too. This is the path Buddha thought, as I understand.

Earlier, we talked about the inputs to the mind from our sensory organs, such as the eye, ear, tongue, skin, and inner mind. In the quest to search for this path to Nirvana, Buddha understood that the abovementioned sensory inputs we capture are forever changing or in flux. However, as soon as the mind gives it an identity, the mind latches on to it even if it changes form immediately. The mind then tries to relate the new image to the old image. If it, does it would update the old image with the new image.

As said before, if this change is observable by us, we tend to think it is the same object, a continuation of the same object, or a phenomenon we experienced before. On the other hand, if this change was not observable for a long time, we may not even recognize this form later. This is because our mind will not be able to match this form with what is in the memory. In consideration of a human, for example, if we see a person after 50-60 years, we may not recognize that person as the same person we knew earlier, even if it's a family member.

In addition, if we go by modern science, every material thing or matter in this universe is made of atoms or a form of energy. Atoms make the tangible matter as us humans, trees, animals, rocks, air, and even water. Energy is mainly in the forms of sound, heat, and light we experience. Atoms are made from smaller entities called subatomic particles, known as electrons, protons, and neutrons. These subatomic particles, in turn, are made up of other smaller particles called mesons, gluttons, etc. And they, in turn, maybe from other smaller particles that we do not know of currently.

In the end, all matter is supposed to manifest waves of energy, which the scientists call 'string theory' according to one school of thought. Hence, every such thing of form in this whole universe is made of energy. We have discussed earlier the scientific proof for this as to how matter becomes heat, light, and sound energy, which we know are in the waveform. As making heat and light, we see on earth from nuclear fusion happening in the sun.

However, not to complicate the matter, we will not talk of antimatter particles that are opposite of the said electrons, protons, etc. If matter and its corresponding antimatter particles collide, the results would be the annihilation of both particles to become nothing but energy. This is another example of matter, where it becomes energy in the end, like nuclear fission, which is the atomic bomb. So much energy is released as heat, light, and sound, and all of it is in the waveform.

If this is so, there is nothing we can call permanent in this world, including our universe, where its contents, such as stars and even whole galaxies, we can observe changing by explosions and then reforming. Hence, in the end, what we experience in this world are energy forms in different manifestations, which our senses say physically exist as we could feel them to our touch and see them from our eyes and even sometimes mold or change them as we want.

Now, what is the situation of proof of wave energy as light, heat, etc., forming matter? This we can abundantly see in our surroundings. For example, plants, which make their food using light energy in a process called 'Photosynthesis.' In this process, light energy becomes part of the plant's food, and this food becomes part of the plant as its leaves, branches, etc., or things with mass. Notwithstanding this, scientists also claim they have created matter by colliding photons of light.

However, as far as we are concerned, the only thing that exists until we die is our self-made identity or what we call 'self' by the continuous reminder to our mind that I am so and so. Unfortunately, people with dementia even lose this identity and may wander around without knowing who they are or where they are.

This is not to say that if somebody hits someone, they do not feel the pain. The thing here is not the physical body that feels the pain, only the mind. So, all our activity in this universe is in the realm of our mind, which we do not know what it is, or where it is in our body, or even whether it is around our body, though we know we can control it. And, of course, this mind does not seem to fit with our earlier said concept of matter and energy as we do not know whether this mind is an energy form or something related to another dimension. To this end, we know that by removing any part of our body, we do not lose our minds. Even removing half of the brain through a medical procedure called 'Hemispherectomy,' we do not lose our mind and maybe some motor function as walking, etc. But then, if the other half is also removed, you would be dead and have no time to find out where the mind is now.

However, people have harvested this power of the mind to set objects on fire without touching them, to bend spoons, read other people's thoughts, travel in space, or project image of themselves far distances. Buddha and some Arahants supposedly have done such things.

The basis for some of this is now proven to be a possibility by the scientists and is called 'Entanglement.' Light we see is supposed to be made from particles called photons. In this scenario, the entangled light particles or split photons of light are then projected to vast distances. Scientists have now found and proven that one of these split photons far away instantaneously responds to any changes made to its other corresponding light photon. So, the question is, did Buddha split the light reflecting on his body or his image and project it far away, showing his mastery of nature's phenomena by his mind? This we may try to prove by corroborating some of his rare utterances of the nature of the universe with what scientists now know.

Another aspect in relation to this is the glow of light around his head, as witnessed by some when he was meditating and interestingly even on the head of other religious icons, also shown in some statues today. We know as per catabolism, or when the body makes energy from food, the body emits heat as a byproduct. Scientists have captured this heat around our body on film and even tried to use it to diagnose illnesses. The point here is, if the heat is so intense, it would partly illuminate as light as fire does. So, does this mean when Buddha meditated, the intensity was so high, meaning his brain used so much energy, people saw this as a light around his head? If so, again, this shows his deep interaction with the space or universe around him by deep meditation.

Then, one may argue as to how it is we can move from one location to the other physically as we experience flying from one country to another. To my thinking, it is only a form of energy that is moved with our mind saying it is a 'self' that has moved in space. To me, trying to understand this is like a fish trying to understand how a rocket moves in space or another medium it cannot fathom. So, is this what we call reality or an illusion?

A good example to this end is the straw in the water we talked about before. We saw the water bending the straw. Now, when we move the straw, its position changes in the water as per what we OBSERVE. But we know it is not the actual position of the straw in the water.

Anyhow, in all this, we have seen the importance of understanding the human mind as Buddha did to keep our economy at 100% or nearest, with whatever pain that may come to our mind. Thus, the importance of getting control of the mind to overcome any obstacle or pain in this life is of great importance than challenging reality, but also know that our mind is the thing that gets affected when this illusion or reality interacts with it.

To me, the mind has two scenarios: the inner mind and the outer mind. Our inner mind, which generates our feelings, as discussed before, we have no idea what it is or where it is. Some think it is in the brain. The only thing we know of this mind is, it changes all the time. And it is possible to take control of it and even interrogate it by oneself using our outer mind. It is a unique human ability, as stated by Buddha.

After considering all this, it seems there is nothing permanent to cling on to 'as mine' even if our mind says things exist physically the way we observe them. Thus, a true understanding of this phenomenon, what we call our existence, is what Buddha said is the way to Arahant status or path to Nirvana, or 100% economy forever.

This true understanding is gained by our ability to interrogate how our own inner mind works by deep meditation. Meditation helps to focus our outer mind on the functioning of our inner mind and, importantly, to take CONTROL of it.

This type of meditation is called 'Vipassana Meditation,' a technique he found that leads to the true understanding of 'self,' which Buddha realized on his own. The way of achieving this, he disclosed in the Sutra 'Mahasatipatthana Sutra.' Buddha used this Vipassana Meditation to realize the truth of what we call living things, the existence or continuation of samsara or the birth and death cycle, and most importantly, the nature of what we call **Karma**.

Meditation had been a practice in India even before Buddha's time. As for the gurus of that time, other than Buddha, their aim had been to achieve a higher state of existence after death and gain the power to travel in space by meditation, etc. But Buddha said even if one achieves the higher state of this existence, it would be of no help in the end as far as ending the birth-death cycle is concerned. This is because they have not got away from the underlying reasons for this birth-death cycle. However, they may go to a good realm of existence temporarily due to this mind development and positive karma it generates.

In the end, one even comes down to hell as one's good karma wanes and bad karma, which may have been committed, takes precedence. However, what distinguishes Buddhist meditation against the Brahmin's mediation had been this vipassana mediation or inward meditation to one's own senses, including the inner mind, as said before. This is for the true understanding of the impermanent and unsatisfactory nature of all what our senses say exists to achieve the Arahant status. This finally leads one to Nirvana after death, never to join this birth and death cycle again.

In this regard, our outer mind is our mind we use to willfully react to our senses, which we use to read books, think about what we read, etc. The inner mind is what triggers our desires and pops messages to us to do things even to the extent of killing, stealing, etc., and, of course, good deeds, such as charity and compassionate deeds. In the case of the book, it is the inner mind that gave us the compulsion to read it and the outer mind to conclude if the book was good or bad per the feeling the inner mind generates after reading the book.

So why do I give so much focus in this book to what he disclosed?

Once Buddha said that he understood more of what is happening in our universe nearly 2600 years ago by taking control and focusing his mind through focused meditation. He illustrated this point by taking a grain of sand and saying to his followers or monks that what he is disclosing is only such an amount and what he knows is like a vast amount of sand. Back then, there were no telescopes, satellites, or deep space probes sending signals to Earth from outer space, to know about all these. For Buddha, it was only his mind to this end.

So, as per his knowledge of the universe, some of his rare quotes are given below. By knowing how the universe works, his focus was to find a path for 100% economic satisfaction for humans in this life and forever, thus, to overcome its hold on us or never to repeat the life-death cycle again. As said earlier, this was by attaining the status of Arahant in mind, leading to Nirvana after death. He then taught how to practice the way to this path to whoever was interested to know about it for them to follow too.

He attained this Arahant status in principle by totally eradicating greed, lust, and ignorance that were some of the key attributes which bind us to this life-death cycle. Hence, almost all his disclosures to us were about how to achieve this mind status and, as said before, and not to explain how the universe works or its origin or where it ends, etc., other than on few occasions.

Again, even though he mentioned the universe in a few instances, his disclosure to us was not to waste time by thinking of where the end of the universe is, etc., when the opportunity is now at hand to end this samsara or birth or death cycle. However, after achieving the state of mind, Arahant, then one would automatically understand the answers to all questions if there is still the need for it for them.

Buddha's teachings were especially for the monks who were expected to live a monastic life or nonattached life, keeping to oneself and spending one's whole life in much mediation. By focusing on oneself to realize how unsatisfactory one's own self and the surroundings, they could achieve 100% economic status and by this true understanding, leading to non-attachment to all, including oneself.

However, this does not mean people, such as astrophysicists or related scientists, should not study space or the universe as an occupation, as they may be able to discover how to deflect an incoming asteroid going to strike Earth or how to find a new habitat for humanity in the event of Earth being in danger of destruction, etc. Humans also could spend an entire life in the quest of how to eliminate certain diseases without a result. All these were ways for living for them or the need to meet economic requirements or in the process of trying for that 100% economic satisfaction. However, at the same time, not forgetting the unsatisfactory nature of this life and devote at least some time to meditation and charity to learn to let go of one's attachments as much as possible.

Earlier, we mentioned that the final stage of the four stages of achieving Arahant or the 100% economic status is when greed, hatred, ignorance, etc. can be totally eradicated with the true understanding of impermanence, dissatisfaction, and self-centeredness that we receive from all the external inputs through our five senses as well as those signals or thoughts coming to our outer mind from our inner mind.

This state of mind of Arahant is mostly achievable by the monks who cultivate the will and practice of specific types of meditation as taught by Buddha and living in celibacy and seclusion to this end in order not to get disturbed by outside events.

As for the laypeople, to my knowledge, this does not mean that they cannot or have not achieved this state of mind if a teacher could tailor-make such teachings to suit one's own condition of mind. Buddha has supposedly done this as he had the ability to read other people's minds and focus his disclosures accordingly.

There is a story on this I found remarkably interesting in this regard. There had been a monk who could not meditate or remember the disclosure Buddha had been giving to practice meditation. So, he came to Buddha and told him of his predicament. Then Buddha gave him a piece of beautiful white cloth and asked him to rub it down, I think, with his hand and then wash the same and repeat the process until he asked him to stop. When the monk did this, he saw this nice piece of white cloth getting dirty and, in the end, get wasted away. This made him realize the unsatisfactory nature of this life, leading him to the first stage of the Arahant ship.

So even after achieving the first stage, some lingering existence of lust, greed, delusion would remain, as experienced by laypeople in this life, their economy would not be 100% but could increase up to this level as they practice Buddha's teachings to the goal of Arahant.

Earlier, we mentioned that Buddha focused his teachings only on what was required for the people to achieve this state of mind of Arahant in this life. He said to try at the least to achieve the first stage of the said four stages now. He said that achieving the first stage would eventually and would lead to the last stage, if not in this life, then in some other life. Also, once you achieve this first stage, you will not go back but forward to the last stage.

He rarely talked on any non-relevant matters to this end, though his knowledge of the happenings of the universe had been much vast as to the cause of rebirth or effect of karma etc., as mentioned earlier. This extent of knowledge is unfathomable to our non-trained deluded minds.

However, on few occasions, he had talked about the universe due to a specific requirement, which scientists are now validating. This should at the least give us some interest to practice what he has disclosed if we wish to have near 100% economic condition in this life. However, trying to validate his disclosures without practicing would be like, an attempt by a first-grade child trying to justify the truth of what Einstein has stated.

Further, confirmation of the depth of his mastery of the universe is apparent by his alleged ability to project his image to vast distances. A few years ago, this statement would have been like an impossibility. Did he use what scientists now call 'Quantum Entanglement' to do this, as explained above? Then, apparently, he could also read other people's minds, travel to other places in the universe, etc. It is also currently known that there are some people who have mind powers to bend spoons without touching them, elevate oneself via deep meditation, etc. All this is done through the concentration of their mind. At the minimum, we sometimes can feel in our mind when someone is staring at us from behind though we do not see that person.

And then there was this lady monk in Vietnam who committed death in protest of foreign occupation by self-immolation after going into deep trance or concentration of the mind, as we saw pictures of this happening in the news media at that time. The point here is she did not even flinch when her body started burning. This tells us that there are things that are associated with our mind as to its power we have no clue about.

To this end, it would be an interesting story related to one of the books in this regard. During Buddha's time, there was this excellent, exceptionally morally good, highly athletic student who studied under one of the teachers. It was the custom at that time for students to pay the teacher at the end of their studies. The teacher then told the student what the payment should be for teaching them. This may be even free labor to work in his fields. One of the other students was jealous of this bright student and lied to the teacher that he was having an affair with someone dear to him. So, with his mind now poisoned, to avenge this intelligent student, the teacher demanded something like a thousand human fingers in a necklace from him as the payment, knowing he would be killed in this process.

Now apparently, the student had no choice but to fulfill the teacher's demand. To this end, he hid in a forest and started killing and cutting the fingers of people passing by. Now the king had come to know about this and had prepared his troops to catch and kill him. The mother of the student now had heard about this and was now planning to go to the forest to save her son.

One early morning, as usual, Buddha was looking at the world from his mind to see who he could help that day. Then he apparently saw what was going to happen to the mother of the student as he would probably kill her to fulfill his obligation to the teacher as he was only missing one finger for this deed now. And though this student had so much good karma to become enlighten, this crime would negate this opportunity for him.

Apparently, he was so focused on what he had to do that this person was not in a frame of mind to reason. So, to save him, Buddha realized the first thing to do was to completely exhaust him physically and as well as mentally to stop this focus he currently has and open his mind to outside. Now to keep the story short, Buddha then **projected** his image in front of him.

Seeing the Buddha, this person had started chasing him to cut his fingers too. However, as soon as he was about to catch up with him, he projected himself further. This happened so many times that, in the end, this guy could not run or walk anymore and shouted out to Buddha to stop. Then Buddha **read his mind** and replied that he has stopped, meaning he had stopped the journey of samsara or birth and death cycle, and whether he has done it too. This simple question apparently brought the student to his senses due to his intelligence, which was now able to manifest in his mind as to what he was doing. This has been so narrated in the story of "Angulimala Sutra" for whoever is interested.

Now we will try to see what the scientist are now saying as per what Buddha had talked about 2600 years ago about the universe. As said before, there were no telescopes, space probes, just his mind and eyes to this end.

"There is monks, an inter-cosmic [1] void, an unrestrained darkness, a pitch-black darkness, where even the light of the sun & moon — so mighty, so powerful — doesn't reach."

-'Andhakara Sutra,' Sutra means Disclosure.

We know this now as we go away from our star system or the sun; it is pitch dark, as our sun rays no longer reach or are so diluted in the cosmic void, the space between the star systems.

Now, we take the statement of one of our most famous scientists, Einstein, who predicted that even light can be bent by gravity and cannot escape such gravity of a black hole, which we know now is at the center of galaxies or a star system. This means that pitch darkness should exist at the center of our galaxies with such black holes in the center. Even as the sun rays would disperse in the vast universe, leaving nothing but the darkness within a star system.

The Buddha once explaining the world system said, **"Monks, as far as sun and moon revolve and illuminate in all directions by their radiance, so far does the thousand-fold world system extend. In addition, in that thousand-fold world system, there are a thousand moons, a thousand suns, inhabited planets...**

This thousand-fold world system is called Minor World-System, which is the smallest unit in the universe".

-'Kosala Sutra'

To me, this statement of 'Minor World-System' is profound, as this describes what we know of the universe today with all the apparatus we currently have, including the Hubble Telescope and other vast arrays of other telescopes looking at different wavelengths of light, X-Ray, etc. coming from space.

We now know that our solar system, consisting of the sun, moon, and planets to be the smallest system in our universe. Our galaxy is made of billions of such solar systems of suns, moons, planets, etc. and billions of such galaxies make up our universe. This is a perfect match to what has been said over 2600 years ago by the sheer concentration of his mind and its focus to understand our existence to the best I can think of.

In another instance, Buddha said, **"Our solar system will come to an end with our star becoming so intense of seven stars, and the heat will destroy all our plant in flames."**

-'Anguttara-Nikaya, 7.66 and "Sattasariyasuttau Sutra"

As per my interpretation of the abovementioned quote, we can now physically see the suns in other solar systems getting brighter and brighter as seen through the Hubble Telescope and then exploding and destroying to smithereens all that is near it and becoming what scientists now call an extremely dense entity called the neutron star.

In another instance, during this time in India, people had a great belief that astrology was responsible for most of the things that happened to them. They devoted much of their lives to appease the planets and stars or the heavenly bodies and gain favors from their effects. To an extent, mostly everything important in their life was done as per their position of planets in the sky. Even today, some people in Asian countries do the same. They follow what we now know as the 'Horoscope.' In this environment, a monk who was obsessed with astrology asked Buddha to explain the effects of stars and planets on humans. As we said earlier, Buddha did not talk about the universe, but for some reason, in this instance, he has responded to this monk by showing and asking him of a star far away.

"Do you believe that star still exists?"

The monk said, "Yes."

Buddha explained to him that we only see the light from this star, and the star no longer exists.

-"Sattasuriyuggamana Sutra"

In consideration of this statement by Buddha, scientists now know this is true. The reason is that stars are billions of miles away from us, and light has a certain speed of propagation. For example, if we consider our nearest star, the Proxima Centauri, its light takes nearly 4.3 light-years to reach us. This means a ray of light emitted at any time from this star now traveling at the speed of light would take 4.3 years to reach Earth or our eye. Does this mean if it was this star, Buddha had been observing millions of visible stars in the sky 24/7 all his life to now this.

Now we know this star is still there. So, Buddha may have been talking of another star further away, meaning whose light would take a much longer period to reach Earth.

Now we know, if such a star explodes, it becomes something else known as a supernova or black hole. Scientists now know all this as they have been monitoring these stars 24/7 for years to see what happens to them using large telescopes of different varieties and high-power computers.

Now Buddha, of course, did not have all that 2600 years ago. Neither one would expect he had nothing to do but look at the sky 24/7 to monitor these rays of light coming from billions of stars in the sky. Now the question is, how did Buddha have such accurate information to make a statement on the nature of this star? To me, this shows his vast knowledge of the working of the universe when he said to his monks that he preaches only a few grains of sand of the mounds of it there is.

As per what has been discussed above, it seems now scientists have talked about planets moving around the suns in the universes. Copernicus, in 1463, said the sun is at the center of our universe.

Galileo, in 1609, discovered the telescope to observe the planets around us. Notwithstanding all this, Buddha had said this nearly 2600 years ago. How he managed to gain such profound knowledge of the universe remains a mystery.

Now, most of us have seen the film 'Star Trek' with the famous phrase of 'Beam me up, Scotty,' where humans get atomized and get sent to another location and get reconstituted. Apparently, now scientists have achieved this on a minute scale. It is said Buddha could achieve this on his own as he had traveled from Northern India to a high mountain peak in Sri Lanka. Had he walked, it would have taken years, not to mention the climb to the peak of that mountain or the need to cross the ocean. A similar feat was achieved by one of his disciples, too, as far as we know.

For writing this book, I have delved a little bit deeper into Buddha's disclosures as it appears these relate directly to the economic well-being of the masses in this life. The profound knowledge of the working of the universe he displayed made me curious to study his disclosures further as the sutra 'Dependent Origination,' which is based on what is known as **Karma** in the teachings of 'Patichcha Samuppadaya Sutra.'

Moreover, most importantly, these disclosures seem to have a scientific foundation, meaning if practiced as said, the results would be immediate in this life, and you won't have to wait to experience them in another life.

As mentioned before, it is also important to note that as per Buddha, his emphasis and teachings were also on how to make our economy 100%. This is by emphasizing how to detach ourselves from what our physical senses and mental thought processes are telling us by understanding that they are impermanent and always changing in nature. Hence, nothing to cling to.

Most importantly, his teaching is self-dependent to achieve objectives in this life and not dependent on others for one's own salvation. In simple words, to keep on trying even if one fails during one's efforts to achieve good or positive objectives. At the same time, not allow our self-ego to affect our self-contentment in pursuit to achieve a 100% economy for ourselves.

In this life, we have many examples of successes of people practicing this principle, especially during Buddha's time. In the end, to achieve Nirvana or the eternal bliss state, thus, avoiding being reborn. Rebirth, as we know now, is a fact. For rebirth to happen, one will still have to go through old age, sickness, and death in this life and then, new life in a mother's womb in total darkness, immersed in a water bubble for many months. Not something to look forward to for me.

To this end, Buddha disclosed what he called the 'Four Fundamental Truths' or 'Four Noble Truths,' as the foundation to all his disclosures as mentioned before, where all these were based on and detailed in nearly fifteen thousand Sutras or disclosures. These were his answers to specific questions asked or similes to illustrate certain fundamental points to his followers as laymen or monks or direct disclosures to them.

Interestingly, he had three ways of answering questions when asked. The first was a direct answer to the question, the second was to give a simile to the person to understand the answer by themselves, and the third was silence. The last was done when the person did not have the mental capacity to understand the answer.

His teachings were mainly to the monks. However, the teachings also included what was required for a peaceful, just society. They are instructions on how a king should govern his kingdom, how a husband should treat his wife, how a wife should treat her husband, duties of children to parents, duties of parents to the children, etc. All this focuses on maintaining harmony in the society we live in, leading to a possible 100% economy for all, physically as well as psychologically.

As per the four noble truths, firstly, life is unsatisfactory, meaning everyone is subjected to aging and will have to face losing loved ones. We are subjected to be associated with people we do not like, get sick and suffer, and ultimately succumb to death. Secondly, the reason for this is our lust or greed and attachment to material things, even food. Thirdly, that there is a way out of this by eradicating greed by the true understanding of our nature. Lastly, the path to follow to achieve this objective is called the 'middle path' or the 'Eight Fold Path' or practices.

It is also important to note that as per Buddha, his emphasis and teachings were on how to make our economy 100% immediately in this life and achieve Nirvana or the state of internal bliss in the end, as said before. This is to do away with being reborn, which is a fact that is acknowledged by many scientists and renowned people, such as Thomas Huxley, Dr. Ian Stevenson, Mahatma Gandhi, Henry Ford, General S. Pattern, and George Harrison, to name a few.

Hence, all his guidance to humanity has been to this end. He rarely spoke about the universe except in a few rare instances, as said earlier. Buddha, in these few instances, spoke extensively about the universe as a 'Kalpa' or 'eon.' To explain this further, an eon would be like the time it would take to smooth out a large rock, such as the Himalaya, to the ground by rubbing it with a cloth, assuming of course that the cloth would not tear off. As we know now, scientists are speaking about billions of years when talking about the birth of this universe or the **Big Bang** theory.

The justification of the Big Bang has been due to some determination by scientists as the discovery of background noise or radiation in the universe, seeming to be equally distributed in all directions when measured apparently from the free atomic particles created during the big bang. Now, this big bang is supposed to be just one of the many big bangs that happened earlier. Consequent to the expansion of the universe, at some point, it is supposed to contract to a single point again. This, in scientific language, is called 'Singularity,' which was already spoken about by Buddha 2600 years ago in '**Agganna Sutra.**'

It is also interesting to mention that Buddha, on one occasion, also mentioned that Earth was once only an ocean without land, and all animals originated from the water. Today, scientists say the same thing, which means they agree to '**Agganna Sutra.**'

The point in all this is that we are talking of some human being who had this wisdom nearly 2600 years ago on this subject. Earlier, we talked about Bachelor's degrees, Master's degrees, and Ph.D. In case of a disagreement among them, whom do we believe? Then we agreed on the Ph.D. as the highest educated on that subject. We know a Ph.D. holder used his outer mind to understand a minuscular thing happening in this world. This may not even prove to be totally accurate or absolute unless more in-depth research is done on the subject.

However, now we know that Buddha understood the universe by focusing on his inner mind to understand that there is a pathway to reach a 100% economic achievement in this life and not wait for the elusive next life for it. He expounded this pathway to everyone who would be interested to hear about it. Not by force, deceit, or bribes, but by spending nearly all his adult life explaining this path that he found through compassion to all, not for personal gain, glory, or self-ego. He lived with what others gave him to eat and had only a few items of material things, such as his eating bowl, two sets of robes, etc. This is against the princely life he left behind to find this path.

In general, what we currently describe as religions do preach good things to their disciples, such as showing compassion to all living beings, including your neighbors, animals, etc., while the Creator or God they represent do not. It's a paradox indeed.

Some religions instruct you to kill animals for food only, using a sharp knife with one stroke. Instructions are also given to eat all you have killed and to give any leftovers to your neighbor without wasting them. You are also required to ask for forgiveness from the Creator as you make this killing for food only.

The underlying message here to me is that if you kill, you should make it painless as possible so that the animal would not suffer and never kill as a sport. In another religion, did not the son attend to the sick when his father made others sick? Then he carried a sheep when it was sick in his arms. Is this going against God's will, or as said earlier, was it the work of the devil and the son eventually paid with his blood to liberate these people from the devil?

Unfortunately, through history, we have not seen the liberation for all that blood sacrificed by the son to the devil. Nevertheless, billboards say he is coming again soon, but perhaps not for the many billions who have died up to now waiting for him.

Another thing of interest is to understand the similarities of the clergy who practice these religions and philosophies. Consider a few mentioned below:

a) Did they not count beads of a necklace? Apparently, this concept of counting the beads originated in India during the time of the Brahmins or people who meditated for their salvation from this unsatisfactory world. This was even used by Buddha when he was initially learning under the best-known teachers at that time to master what they knew. In the end, he knew he had to find this path by himself as what he learned was not what he expected in this regard.

   Now counting of beads, the mind is concentrated in the counting process, where no other thoughts are directed to the mind, giving a sense of peace and tranquility to that person.
b) The faithful of these beliefs seem to go around objects they venerate. And they do this only three times or seven times.
c) They all seem to wear white clothes and cover their bodies, meaning no shorts, no short skirts, or too exposed body parts when visiting locations they pray or venerate at.
d) Some have white cloth also strung on their left shoulder.
e) Generally, they wash and clean themselves first before they do these rituals.
f) The priests related to these beliefs do not get married, especially in the old days, or follow celibacy.

g) All these priests do some sort of meditation or practice of self-control.
h) They all talk of compassion, even to the animals.
i) They all talk of do's and don'ts for the harmony of society.
j) Especially in the old days, the priest shaved their heads, maybe to show no identity as an army does to the soldiers.
k) They all expound the virtue of human cleanliness to the point of keeping one's self-clean, including the floor of the house.
l) All these religions and Buddhism have the concept of confession. In Buddhism, the objective is not forgiveness of one's sins which will not happen per this philosophy but admit to the same in front of another senior monk and accept his correct guidance and forgiveness.

   So, what is the reason for this confession in Buddhism? A confession stops one from thinking about a bad deed repeatedly. This falls into the Buddhist doctrine of "the thought is prime to initiate karma." Meaning, if you think of a bad deed you did, on and on, this itself leads to bad karma to a degree, though no consequent related action has been done. Similarly, if you keep on thinking of good deeds you did and cherish them, it generates positive karma, though you only have done it one time.
m) Interestingly, in Buddhism, too, there is something like what other religions call 'Born Again.'

This is when one accepts Buddha's disclosures and makes a new determination to practicing positive karma or good deeds, and avoids negative karma or bad deeds. In this way, there is a possibility that some of the repercussions of negative karma may not get an opportunity to manifest in that person in this life or another life.

Sometime after the passing of Buddha, one of his disciples named Nagasena was trying to explain certain Buddhist concepts to an Indo-Greek king, as was illustrated in the books titled 'MilindaPrashnaya' or 'Milinda Panha.'

One of the questions the king asked was how it is possible to avoid the effects of bad karma. The disciple then said to the king, as I understand, if a boat is made of a large rock, which we can call good karma, and if there are small rocks, say bad karma, in it, will the boat sink in its journey of life? The king said no. Then the disciple said, this is how you balance the effects of bad karma. And it is the other way around with good Karma.

Irrespective of the said similarities above, there are some notable differences, among them is circumcision, which is cutting off a body part. Don't you think that cutting a part of a man's body, which God created, is going against the God of creation? On the other hand, did the Creator come to someone and ask this be cut off as he made a mistake, and now it made the man unclean in no time? In addition, why did God not figure this out at the time of creation?

Notwithstanding this, when there's the need for the doctors to save a person's life by cutting part of the body created by God when they go bad and gangrene sets in when a body part dies and starts rotting or when there's the need to remove a body part, say due to cancer, then you may ask the question, who God is now? Or will these doctors now go to hell for this? Or any of the most aberrant devotees now say, please leave this body part as it was given to me by the Creator. Of course not. They would only clamor to get rid of it and become well again.

Fair treatment in the least was expected to all at the time of birth, as newborns have not had the opportunity to believe in Him or know about Him. However, some are given privileges at birth by being born to loving and kind families with all the needs provided, while some at a tender age of few years see their parents die of lingering diseases, such as HIV, cancer, etc. in front of their eyes and end up helpless. Eventually, they themselves would die of starvation or disease, as we see happening in Africa. Nevertheless, are we all not supposed to be equal in the eyes of God? Is this because God is powerless in this situation, as the devil made this world?

Did these prophets, wise and noblemen, influenced by ancient philosophies from India, try to discipline their flock as kings do so that society could exist and be compassionate even to animals? For example, as said before, they preach to keep the floor of the house clean first, which prevents the spread of diseases. In addition, not to eat from dusk to dawn for a period of time in the year in order to learn to control one's own desires and even prohibit the swallowing of one's saliva during this period. Also, they dictate that one should give to charity to help the needy in order to develop compassion in one's mind. As a king, he would then order his soldiers to punish those who did not follow his dictates.

Conclusion

From everything that we have discussed in this book, in the end, one can consider the economy to be 100% to a person or persons only if they are content with what they have now. This is, even when they are facing the most adverse situations, such as starvation, but still decides to be positive. To achieve this, they should be able to give up everything they have and be attached to nothing in this physical world. However, it would be only a very few who would manage to achieve this status as an individual. Nevertheless, for the survival of humans or society, it is profoundly required for the people to find the means to increase the quality of life one notch at a time with new inventions, new food sources, etc. In the same token, the rich will not have their economy well for them or even near 100% if they spend all their time under stress, trying to obtain more earthly possessions. This is because a person would leave behind everything they own, including what that person wears, in the end, and as per some, only carry their good or bad deeds to wherever they are going in the end.

Earlier, I mentioned I would rather say his disclosures than teachings. On the other hand, if he was a teacher, then he would be the supreme teacher ever to exist in all generations of humans we know of, as he thought facts or Dhamma or the way of the universe which was absolute and not subjected to the consequent need of variations, modifications, or changes with new insight to our nature, for example as science does. Then how to beat any agony of this nature on us for 100% economic satisfaction now and forever?

So finally, a person's economy lies in their minds, but for a community, the economic activity must go up at least one notch at a time to keep all members hopeful even if the economy is not 100% currently.

In conclusion, I thought it would be pertinent to mention a couple of quotes by Buddha, documented in the old Indian language of Pali, translated to English by me to the best of my understanding of their meaning as I think they relate to the topic of this book.

Health Is The Best Profit One Can Have
Contentment Is The Best Wealth On Can Posses
Good Friends The Best Comfort One Can Have
Nirvana Is The Eternal Bliss One Can Achieve
(to me 100% economy)

A person who thinks he is contented has the whole world to enjoy
(My Take: Who is contented has nothing to grab onto and can now enjoy positives of the world while they last)

References

Thanks To:

Wikipedia and Google for research on some subject matter. And for Pictures – https://images.app.goo.gl/b4ton4Wprrv4k8oS6